The Extermination of Big Barney Sahs

Crime and Murder in America's Prohibition Era

Written by: Edward August Gartz
Editor: Meg Myers

You will know most of the people in this book. Eddie

The Extermination of
Big Barney Sahs

Crime and Murder in America's Prohibition Era

Prologue:

This story is about the Prohibition Era. It is based on facts told to me by my Uncle Cornelius Steimer who passed away at the Hamilton Manor Nursing Home in Rochester, New York in 1998 at the age of 91. Uncle Neil's days of crime started when he was young. Before he turned 21 he owned a Rochester, New York speakeasy and gambling club directly across from New York State Railways that operated trolley buses until 1938 when the Rochester Transit Company was established. Uncle Neil was my mother's sister Betty's second husband. Although quite a character Uncle Neil treated me like gold while he was quite hard on many others. After I learned how his father treated him I understood why he had some personal failings. I learned a great deal about the Prohibition Era from Uncle Neil, who told me about actual events he experienced at his club. One gambler's wife showed up at the door demanding that Neil return the money that the guy had lost that afternoon. It surprised the heck out of me to learn how he handled this situation. One of the behaviors I had learned about my Uncle was that a dollar and my Uncle were not soon parted. He would hold onto a dollar so tight he'd displace the ink. So I was shocked to hear him say, "I had to shut her up or she'd go to the police so I gave her back every dollar she was demanding right then and there. I banned her husband from gambling at the club from that day on. He'd stop for a beer quite often but gambling was out. He was a danger because he couldn't control his wife."

Uncle Neil loved beer but didn't like to gamble. He told me that he'd sit in and play poker only if there weren't enough patrons, just to keep the game going. He'd play only until another gambler showed up and then he'd give up his seat to the new player. The idea was to keep the game going because he'd get a percentage of every pot.

There were some real Rochester mob figures who were frequent patrons at his club. One hot night there was a disturbance coming from teens playing in a pool outside the clubs open windows. A couple of wise guys who were exceptionally poor losers blamed their losses on not being able to concentrate because of the noise. They dealt with that by coming back that night and completely trashing the pool to assure the noise would not be there the next night.

Mob figures also offered to handle debt collection for Uncle Neil if he was owed money from patrons from whom he had floated loans. He told me that he stopped giving loans because if patrons didn't want to pay him back he'd lose both the patron and his money. Therefore, Uncle Neil never had to avail himself of their collection services. He was hard on people but he didn't want to have their legs or arms broken.

One of the oddest stories he told me was about a few of the trolley and bus drivers who had the practice of stealing fares received from riders. Uncle Neil pulled out a quarter to demonstrate. He said it went like this, "If the driver received a large coin like a fifty cent piece they'd flip it into the air and if it stayed up they'd give it to the company, but if it fell back down they'd keep it." I remember seeing the picture in my mind of a trolley driver testing each half dollar coin. You never know when gravity might change.

Yes, Rochester, New York was a very active and dynamic place to live or visit in the Prohibition Era. As you read the story you will hear of local landmarks in the town of Irondequoit, a suburb of Rochester and a portion of Irondequoit called Sea Breeze. This is the setting for much of the story. You will also have the chance to learn about and take "The Ghost Walk" of Sea Breeze where you'll learn much more about its rich history. Then it will be up to you and your thoughts to sort out truth from fiction in the Prohibition Era of Rochester.

I hope in some small way I am giving back to the town of Irondequoit I loved so much. To this day I still travel miles just to take a nostalgic walk through the streets, woods, fields, golf courses and trails that surround the town. I was born and raised in the town of Irondequoit and have a great love for its beauty. I was very fortunate to grow up surrounded by Durand Eastman Park, Irondequoit Bay, Lake Ontario, Seabreeze Amusement Park, and all the wonderful people that call Irondequoit their home. Irondequoit is one of the many fabulous places to live in upstate New York. I encourage all who live in any part of the greater Rochester area to just take a break and reflect on how fortunate we are to call upstate New York our home. We are so fortunate.

This is a fictional account of people and events written just for fun. Any resemblance to people living or dead is purely coincidental.

The Extermination of Big Barney Sahs

Crime and Murder in America's Prohibition Era

The Adventure Begins

In my wildest thoughts and dreams I never could have imagined how a lazy summer day in Rochester, New York could have taken such a dramatic turn and start me on a remarkable adventure that would play out over the next ten years. This journey would lead me down a trail to face one of Rochester's most notorious criminals and would allow me to witness events that to this day have no earthly explanation.

The year was 1922 and I was in my eighth year in the Coast Guard. I was assigned to the Rochester, New York Coast Guard Station on the mouth of Genesee River. My name is Edward August and I joined the Navy during the Great War with hopes of serving in Europe. When the war ended, I transferred to the Coast Guard. Although the dangers of war had long past the danger in my job as a Coast Guard Captain was getting worse every day. Prohibition was in full swing and the demand for illegal alcohol was greater than ever and on the rise. Rumrunners, whisky peddlers, beer and moonshine makers, even pirates were traveling Lake Ontario hauling their forbidden cargos from the shores of Canada to the pubs and speakeasies in the United States. Tommy guns, rifles, revolvers, grenades, and firebombs were the weapons of choice used by all of the scoundrels trying to race across the lake with their illegal cargo. It was our job to stop them and they would do anything to make sure they wouldn't get caught. Our failure would amount to their success and the stakes were very high.

My life in years past was surrounded by sea battles, killing the enemy in numbers when we'd sink a German U-boat or risking imminent death when we were being targeted by the enemy. It was my past that gave me an immense appreciation for life. This particular day was one of those summer days dreams are made of. It was warm and peaceful with a slight breeze and the smell of flowers and fresh cut grass was in the air. It's very strange how life works though. At the precise time I was taking in the beauty in my life, a Rochester family was experiencing the terror that the evildoers of this world can deliver. No one at that time could have known what was going on 30 miles out on Lake Ontario. The Peter Pundt family was slowing their new yacht down to offer help to people they thought were stranded. It was their last stop in life.

Late that afternoon my crew and I were on a routine patrol far out on Lake Ontario. We were still doing sea trials of Rochester's newest Coast Guard Cutter. It wasn't brand new but it was new to us and the best ship we ever had at our station. It was a refit with all the latest technologies. It had two new powerful engines and was equipped with three-inch cannons placed fore and aft. We hadn't planned on making any stops but we spotted what we suspected might be typical rumrunners. Rumrunners were known to be a snobby group of lads. Most were connected into the Boston mobs and Irish high society and many used extremely fast yachts. They had money and powerful connections in the mob and in government. This bunch had one of the newest and fastest yachts I had ever seen. Their yacht was a bit over the top fancy even for the Irish mob, I thought. They didn't attempt to escape when they spotted us so we settled in to what we were sure would be a routine inspection. "This will be an easy one," my first mate uttered. "They look very willing to allow us on board." I was sure he was right. After all, when they saw us coming they just slowed and drifted to a dead stop. We could see from a distance that the crew appeared to be tossing things overboard but we were too far away to know for sure.

As we pulled parallel I got on the megaphone and yelled, "Ahoy there, turn to and prepare to be boarded. You are required by law to yield to the authority of the United States Coast Guard for a routine inspection." As we pulled alongside I called out, "Who is captain of this vessel?" A gentleman stepped out from the bridge, "I'm Captain." "What's your name sir?" "Captain Hetko, Captain Mitch

Hetko at your service." Captain Hetko met me at the gangway, "Nice to meet you, I'm Captain Edward August of the United States Coast Guard. Before we start our inspection can I inquire sir? What were you tossing overboard as we approached your ship?" "We were tossing over cement blocks," he replied. "We used them to weight the bow so we could test the yacht's top speed when hauling capacity loads. We finished the test so we were chucking the blocks over before returning to port. I did this to save on fuel. I hope that's not against the law?" "I don't think so, at least not to my knowledge," I responded.

My crew boarded the yacht and found no contraband on board but they did find something suspicious. The crew found a large stain of what looked like blood in one of the forward compartments and Captain Hetko had no immediate explanation. "Perhaps the blood was left over from a fishing trip that was taken over last weekend," he guessed. "I made the mistake of loaning my new yacht to my brother for a fishing trip and he left it a mess. You know how inconsiderate siblings can be some times, eh Captain?"

After finding out that Captain Hetko did not have his ownership papers or registration on hand we decided to maintain custody of the yacht. We also had to detain Captain Hetko and his crew. We would investigate this further once we were on shore. It could be Captain Hetko had left the paperwork at home as he stated but we had to find out for sure. Given the present state of lawlessness on the lake we adhere very strictly to the law in this matter. This group of sailors didn't seem like a bad lot but I had no choice. I'd let them go as soon as we got back to port. We'd continue to hold their yacht and I'd have to give Captain Hetko a citation for lack of registration papers. He'd have 24 hours to produce them to avoid a rather substantial fine and to get his yacht back.

Not finding any other infractions we decided to leave. Our batteries were low from running our spotlights as the sun went down. I feared if we tried to start the ship we might not be successful and that would reduce the battery power even more. I ordered that the auxiliary gas powered generator be started. In a short time the batteries will recover their charge. It's the penalty you pay for running the lights without the ships engines running. I knew I was being overly cautious but it was a beautiful night and we had the duty for five more hours. Therefore, to assure a clean start I decided to just drift and let the batteries charge for a while. It was the need to charge the batteries that lead us down the path to discover how far men would go to make money and how dangerous this dirty bootlegging business was, especially the farther out from shore one gets.

As I sat watching the stars come out I couldn't help thinking how beautiful the universe is. Looking back, I remember reflecting on how great our God must be to have created such vast beauty and I wished that it would be given to man someday to travel the stars. My rapture this night was soon checked by the noise coming from the stateroom where we were holding the men we had detained. So I walked down and poked my head in and questioned one of my crew. "What's the fuss all about?" "Captain, they're pretty darn upset that we are detaining them." "Perhaps they don't understand that not having their registration papers is a very minor matter?" "Yes Captain, I explained that but that didn't settle them down." Suddenly Captain Hetko pushed his way forward and shouted, "Captain August, when the hell are we getting underway?" I called out to everyone, "Gentlemen, if any of you have a date tonight with some young lovely I'm afraid you won't be making it on time." It was then I realized that Captain Hetko was extremely distressed. His anger seemed to intensify when he recognized we had no plans to allow him or his crew back on their yacht. I reassured them that their yacht was safe and that I had placed two of our best men on it to pilot it back. "I don't give a damn about the yacht I just want to get going," yelled Captain Hetko. "I'm sick of being out here."

Thinking back I could have simply issued a citation for lack of registration and overlooked the lack of ownership papers but that bloodstain in the cabin gave me an eerie feeling in my gut. Added to this I now saw irrational anger in Captain Hetko and his crew. My suspicions were on the rise and this changed my strategy that night. The insistence by Captain Hetko that we get underway jogged my memory of a lesson taught to me in the past.

The lesson came from a friend Cy Hamilton who told me about the time he stopped a ship for a routine inspection. It was just one of Cy's funny but true stories he told at lunch one day. Cy's full name and title was Chief Petty Officer Cyril G. Hamilton. Before Cy retired he had toured the world and had seen action in two wars. As usual Cy laughed and laughed as he regaled us with his story. "One night my crew and I spotted a small craft speeding across some very heavy waves. Their skipper seemed to be risking everything to get to port as fast as his ship would carry him. We signaled them to stop and then pulled alongside for an inspection. We were greeted with smiles and a handshake. All we found on board was a filthy deck with rock salt scattered all over. It was ground into the deck, scattered about the cabin and it was in all the cracks and crevasses, even on the seats. "Are you guys transporting rock salt?" "Sure," he replied, "From time to time I get a load from a friend at the coal towers down by Oklahoma Beach. I use it to keep the driveway clear of ice in the winter and sell a bit to my friends and neighbors." "Now I ask you guys why should we have questioned that?" Cy remarked. "It's Rochester after all and we have some very tough winters. I thought of placing an order myself if the price was right."

Cy continued, "I had the weekend duty and after chow we went back out on patrol but all was quiet. I had the engines off and we sat drifting and enjoying a few cold beverages left over from before prohibition began," Cy chuckled and winked, "One of my men saw the same ship we had inspected earlier heading back out on the lake. It stopped about a mile or two off shore. Then a group of lights coming from the ship lit up the area where they were. The lake was now very calm so we moved in slowly to see what they were doing. One of the bad things about lighting up an area is that it's very hard for those inside the lighted area to see out of the circumference of the lights. Not a smart move if you're doing something illegal. Therefore, we were able to pull in very close. Suddenly we saw boxes popping up from the deep, first one, then another, then another, and another like popcorn in a kettle until they had recovered about 25 of these prizes sent up from Davey Jones Locker. Where the hell were these boxes coming from, what was in them, and who was sending them up from the deep, we wondered? But we sat biding our time and watched this circus play out. I call it a circus because two of the guys fell overboard, the boxes got stacked too high and fell back into the water and the crew was arguing so loudly you could have heard them back at the beach. They were the dumbest criminals I had ever seen.

We watched long enough and then it was time to move in and see just what was in those boxes. You guessed it, booze, bottles and bottles of the stuff, many already broken but we had hit a white lightning, beer, and whisky gold mine on board this small ship. It turned out that they packed their booze in boxes of rock salt. They weren't total dummies, earlier in the day when they saw us coming they simply tossed their cargo overboard. The weight of the rock salt sank the boxes. When the rock salt dissolved the boxes would pop back to the surface and they'd be there to retrieve them. It was their bad luck that we spotted them picking up their contraband after the rock salt dissolved. It was a great plan but foiled when we spotted them all lit up. I tell ya, those poor boys were in tears. I think they had lost a great deal of money and none of them looked like they had two pennies to rub together. It was no surprise they all were unable to make bail before trial." Cy shook his head and chuckled, "Some fellas just shouldn't become criminals."

Getting back to our current situation, I remembered the story Chief Petty Officer Hamilton had told me. I started putting two and two together. When considering how anxious Captain Hetko was to get going and the fact that we had seen them tossing something overboard earlier, I told my crew that we'd stay longer and why. We set out a watch on every key point of the ship. Hours passed and then pop there's one case, then another and another, just like Cy had seen years ago. We stayed to retrieve all the boxes we could. The boxes were big and the bottles were too. This seizure was extremely valuable. Thousands of dollars of all types of whisky and every bottle had the label of a horse riding a lightning bolt. I had never seen that label before so it might be from a new bootlegger. One bottle would keep a drunk happy all day, yet this stuff was pure poison to an alcoholic. I started thinking about the families ruined by alcohol abuse and the many it would kill by poisoning livers, kidneys, eyes, and legs. I've even seen drunks die by falling asleep in their cars and freezing to death in the winter. The worst problem I've seen is drunk drivers crashing their trucks or cars because they're too smashed to drive. They always seem to kill innocent men women and children yet survive themselves. How do they live with themselves after, they must have nightmares for life? I have always wondered why anyone would give in to such a devastating addiction. I for one never liked the taste so I could never comprehend its attraction.

All this was running through my head as I watched the boxes pop up when suddenly I heard one of my men let out a chilling scream. He had tossed in a grappling hook tied to a line and pulled a box in. As it got closer he realized that the hook had lodged in the neck of a body that had come up caught on one of the boxes. There were chains on the body but the buoyancy of the box and the corpse allowed the body to float up to the surface. I was sure now that the bloodstain found on the yacht was most likely from the man who had just floated up.

When we got him on board it was obvious that he had two fatal gunshot wounds. This man had been shot to death and then shot again just to be very sure he was dead. One of my crew, 1st Class Petty Officer Doug Myers thought he recognized the man. "Hey, that's Peter Pundt the Pickle King." "Who is it Myers?" "You know the guy that has the funny ads in the newspaper, 'Don't Be Fickle Buy Peter Pundt Pickles.' That explains why the yacht is named "Dill". He's also a champion fisherman and a great baseball player in the town of Irondequoit, sir."

The body was starting to bloat and it was obvious that we'd have to get the coroner to determine the cause of death and give us a positive identification. We kept this find from the men we were holding and their Captain and quickly got underway. They saw us retrieving the booze earlier so we told them that they would be held for possession and transport of an illegal substance. That seemed to be okay with them and as we got underway even Captain Hetko seemed to settle down. Apparently they all were concerned that the weights holding down the dead man might fail and that's the real reason they were so anxious to leave the area.

When we were back in port I called the police and waited for backup and then had all of them arrested for murder. We then went through the yacht with a fine-toothed comb. We pulled panels off and seats out and we discovered handguns, rifles, and dynamite. Later I had the ownership of the yacht checked. As suspected multi-millionaire Peter Pundt owned the yacht. The coroner also gave us a positive ID as Peter Pundt. After investigating this further we learned that Peter Pundt's entire family was missing. Days later we recovered three more bodies. All persons had been tommy-gunned and tossed overboard. They were Peter Pundt's wife, whom many called Katy Georgia and his sons Mike and Chris. They were found much farther out than Mr. Pundt and had no chains on them or evidence they had ever been weighted down.

It's most likely that the Pundt family had stopped to help what appeared to be a ship in distress. They were then overpowered and the pirates split up the Pundt family leaving Mr. Pundt on his ship to chart and pilot the way to the Port of Rochester. My guess is that Mr. Pundt never realized that his family was murdered as soon as the "Dill" got out of sight. We have no evidence to tie anyone to these murders other than the bodies. We knew most likely others were involved because the three bodies we found had been shot with a tommy gun and we didn't find that type of weapon on the "Dill". Whoever killed the wife and children of Peter Pundt were still at large, and for now they have gotten away with murder. The same can't be said for the group that we caught on Mr. Pundt's yacht. After a very short trial and only three hours of deliberations the jury found them guilty and the judge sentenced them to hang. They would find judgment and I was on hand to see the sentence carried out.

Every first-time criminal should have to attend a hanging. Who knows it might reduce the number of murders. I wondered that day what might be going through the minds of those men as they awoke knowing it was their last day on earth. You could see the fear on their faces as they walked to the gallows. They walked slowly and you could see their knees wobbling and buckling from time to time. As they reached the top two of them fell to their knees and sobbed with their foreheads touching the floor in front of them. Then they were lifted to their feet and each condemned man was moved down the platform. As they reached their place on the platform, the minister stopped to say a word or two to each one of them. With their heads hung down a noose and hood were slipped over each head. Anyone close enough to the platform could hear the whimpering and cries coming from the condemned. As the trap doors were released and the bodies started falling I wondered if any one of them held remorse for their crimes. The kicking went on for minutes for most. Judgment was imparted.

In stark contrast there was a wonderful memorial service at the beautiful German church, Salem United Church of Christ. It was a gorgeous setting for the final farewell service to Rochester's Pickle King and his family and was attended by thousands. Sadly this service also marked the end of the Peter Pundt Pickle Products. They faded into obscurity within a few years and Rochester never had a better pickle for only a nickel.

As bad as these murderers were the worst of the worst criminals in the Rochester area was Big Barney Sahs. He owned a speakeasy and gambling joint on Culver Road in the town of Irondequoit. Big Barney was paying off most of the cops on the beat in that area. Dirty money flowed like beer on a Saturday night at Big Barney's as payola to influence people with power. A few hundred bucks paid to a few cops and a few thousand paid to the town judge was all it took to keep Big Barney in business and money was no object for Big Barney. It was common knowledge that Big Barney had a stash of millions and he had a great deal of help creating that wealth.

To the best of our knowledge Big Barney had two partners. Both were his brothers, both were thugs and both played an important role in Big Barney's business. Big Barney's brothers were really only half-brothers. Their father had five wives and four sons, the brothers appeared to be close. The only exception was one brother who disappeared years before and had never been heard from since. The oldest brother was Neil "the Squeal", known for his skill in finding other speakeasies and then tipping off the police. Neil would find some honest church going person to tip off the cops without them ever realizing they were being used as a patsy by Neil to help Big Barney's business.

If he wasn't searching for other speakeasies Neil "the Squeal" was out putting the squeeze on booze suppliers to get the best price for Big Barney. Neil was never able to do that with one bootlegger named Maximillian "Bop" Lounsbury. Even at Big Barney's Restaurant patrons demanded Lounsbury Liquor so Bop Lounsbury would just threaten to shut down to force Neil "the Squeal" to quit messing with him. Lounsbury and his partner Jeff Shelly manufactured fabulous liquor at a secret location. He hauled his liquor by boat to Lake Bluff beach. They'd transport it using a Water Authority wagon to the Water Payment Office where they both worked. They supplied Big Barney with thousands of bottles but then made the mistake of expanding to supply other speakeasies in the city of Rochester. Neil "the Squeal" found out and within two weeks Lounsbury was in jail and Jeff Shelly was found floating face down in Heidi's Pond near Durand Park. A fishing accident was the official cause of death. Most thought Jeff Shelly was leaned on but fought back. Fighting back was always a huge mistake when dealing with anyone from Big Barney's team of thugs.

Big Barney's little brother was Felton "the Fiend" and he was the money handler and the family thief. He'd steal anything, even from his own mother and was known for doing just that. A few years back he stole all of his mother's stocks, money and jewelry, leaving his mom and his little sister Edna's family to fend for themselves during times of great hardship. Nothing would stop Felton "the Fiend" from stealing anything by hook or by crook. Money, jewelry, cars, stocks and bonds were all targets and Felton "the Fiend" would help himself to everything he could get his hands on.

Yes, Big Barney Sahs and his brothers were evil. They wanted money and power and were getting it by taking over the Town of Irondequoit. The town was made up of many wonderful families from all over the world. Ethnic names like Reetz, D'Aurelio, Olesiuk, Habes, Houlihan, Korneliusen, Siwicki, Stiewe, Norris, and Amadeo. All of these names and many more made up the telephone book. But all the families knew the reputation of Big Barney's establishment and stayed away, especially at night.

The phone number, Hopkins 7-8404, was on the tongue of every man and woman who wanted to get in on the action at Big Barney's. It was the number to call to get reservations at table #711. This table was next to a door that led to a set of stairs and a secret hallway. At the end of the hallway was the gambling casino and bar with all types of favored booze.

This was the way Big Barney controlled the admission to the casino room. If they heaped all the customers who reserved table #711 each night, one on top of the other, they'd stick out well over the top of the building. I admit that would have looked darn funny, especially with one of the chubby gamblers on top.

Competition was keen to get reservations at table #711. The rich and famous and the big gamblers would slip a few dollars to the headwaiter and their names would go on the permanent list. That list was for the special customers and Big Barney had many, many special customers from all over New York State. Big Barney could even count on famous friends who would come in from all over the country. Chicago and New Orleans were the most fashionable destinations for drinkers and gamblers but Big Barney drew a crowd from the trendiest places on earth. Yes, the biggest gamblers in the world and even stars of the silver screen could be seen at Big Barney's.

Knowing the entire story of Big Barney and his brothers you'd wonder why anyone would want to call them friends. As with any of the well-known gangsters most knew that Big Barney's rise to riches was full of crime. Witnesses of their escapades would be paid off or just disappear. Looking back at Big Barney's path it was littered with dead bodies and misery that he and his brothers caused for so many people.

The police tried their best to nail them but lacked witnesses or solid proof of their crimes.

It seemed that my entire life from my earliest days in school, my college education, service in the Navy and then as a Captain in the Coast Guard was all leading me on a collision course with Big Barney, one of the most notorious criminals on earth. Little did I know that the night we found the body of Peter Pundt the Pickle King would become a pivotal night in my life.

It was ten years later in 1932 when I was assigned to attend a meeting and become part of a joint FBI, Irondequoit Police, and Coast Guard undercover operation. At this meeting I met FBI Special Agent Gary W. Rigoni. Agent Rigoni was assigned to capture and shut down Big Barney's operation. Agent Rigoni was from the Buffalo district but took orders out of the FBI office in New York. I also learned at this meeting that there were two undercover FBI agents who had infiltrated Big Barney's operation. These agents were in deep cover and if they were found out they would be in grave danger or possibly in a deep grave. No one on our team knew the identity of the undercover agents not even Agent Rigoni. Communication with the undercover agents was done by notes hidden in old cigar butts and dropped near a trash receptacle at the side entrance where all employees took breaks from their work. The color of the cigar band would alert the sender and receiver. Dark brown would go to the agents in Big Barney's. Light brown would be from the Agents in Big Barney's. To the unknowing observer the cigar butt would look like litter. To the recipient it would be litter to pick up and then make it appear they tossed it into the trash.

As the meeting progressed I had the honor of meeting Sir Donald Kuhman, former agent for Scotland Yard. Sir Kuhman was knighted by Queen Victoria in 1890 for solving one of the biggest murder cases in London since Jack the Ripper. The FBI's New York City office sent Sir Kuhman to Rochester to assist us and consult on the latest investigating techniques. When our meeting concluded I had my assignment as part of a complicated plan that was set in motion that night.

The plan put in place had three main thrusts. FBI Special Agent Rigoni directed the operation and handed out all of the assignments. Agent Rigoni stated that first we would gather information on every person coming and going from the secret room. This assignment would be under the direction of Sir Donald Kuhman. Sir Kuhman was unknown in Rochester and would blend right in as one of the out of town patrons of Big Barney's. Sorting out who was a customer of the speakeasy and who was just a customer of Big Barney's restaurant wouldn't be easy. Many people went in and out of Big Barney's but not everyone got into the secret room where the booze and casino were. Some people went to Big Barney's for dinner and music in the main restaurant and never joined the illegal activity behind the secret door. Knowing the clients who went in and out of the speakeasy portion of Big Barney's might also go a long way towards finding his suppliers.

The gamblers and suppliers were being targeted by our team for arrests and shut down. But the main target was Big Barney, his brothers, and the wise guys who worked for him. It was very important that we get the entire gang in order to end their dominance in Irondequoit and the Rochester area. To release this community from the danger of Big Barney's business it was imperative that we shut this speakeasy down permanently and jail everyone involved.

The second segment of the plan was to find out just who the policemen and judges were who have been protecting Big Barney, his two brothers, and their operation. That part of the plan was given to Chief Dennis Swetz of the Irondequoit Police. Chief Swetz and I had crossed paths in the past. My impression of him was that he was an exceptionally nice guy dedicated to his job. To assure he was not on the take himself the FBI investigated Chief Swetz. He had a few very minor skeletons in his closet. They found he liked to place a few small bets on the local basketball and football games. He was, nevertheless, found to be a great husband and father and an honest person who tried his best to keep law and order in the town of Irondequoit. Years had gone by and Chief Swetz was still fighting an uphill battle against Big Barney's operation. He never seemed to be able to get the evidence needed to arrest Big Barney because every time he'd try to raid the casino it always seemed that Big Barney was being tipped off. Once in a while they'd pick up some two-bit thug or some drunk stumbling around but never the big guy, never Big Barney.

Special Agent Rigoni assigned part three to me. It was years later I learned that the FBI had investigated my life before I was invited to join the team. Since then I wondered what skeletons they had found in my closet. Perhaps they learned that I have an addiction to hot dogs and golden brown french-fries or that as a boy I'd swipe a few apples and grapes from the local farmer. One nice day I wanted to test my new lawn mower so I snuck into a neighbor's yard and mowed it without asking permission. The neighbor was very upset. I must have cut the grass too close. All kidding aside I guess my biggest fault was that a few times a year on very warm days our Coast Guard Cutter was used more for fishing, swimming and picnicking than for patrol. I don't think anyone ever found out about that because given the distance that we'd go out from shore you'd have to have one hell of a telescope to see us.

In any case Special Agent Rigoni gave me my assignment, "Captain August your mission is to focus in on bootleggers coming across the lake in large ships." Special Agent Rigoni determined that it was not in our best interest to stop the small boats because the volume of booze required at Big Barney's was too much to be hauled the 70 miles across from Canada by small boats. Therefore, to find the distribution channel we'd have to investigate the ships big enough to manage high volume shipments.

Additionally, I was also assigned to work with Sir Kuhman to surround Big Barney's with a series of surveillance posts that would allow us to watch for vehicles moving product in and out of Big Barney's delivery bays. My men were assigned to the north side of Big Barney's including the shore of Lake Ontario and Culver Road leading up too Big Barney's from Webster, New York. Culver Road was the only main road heading up to Big Barney's from the town of Webster, Lake Ontario, and Irondequoit Bay so we had the smaller portion of the surveillance operation. Even if criminals decided to pull a ship right up on shore or use the Hojack Railway Line that skirted the lake or even the Local Streetcars that skirted the bay they would still need to transfer the goods to be hauled up Culver Road. But of all the places we had to watch we paid special attention to the area in Webster known as Oklahoma Beach. We knew that was a favored dropping off point for the whiskey peddlers. Sir Kuhman had it much harder because of the number of streets coming south to north towards Big Barney's. Deliveries could be routed through many small streets and held temporarily at homes then delivered covertly at night.

The operation was in full swing when, at an update meeting, Chief Swetz reported that to date they had uncovered one corrupt judge and four dirty cops. They had not arrested them but had them under surveillance to determine if there was anyone else involved. This was done in accordance with our operational plan. This operation was turning into an enormous chess game and any move on one piece, especially a low level pawn might tip off Big Barney. Therefore, it was necessary that we not move on any criminals we exposed. Our goal was to checkmate Big Barney, his men, and everyone connected to his filthy business. So the corrupt judge was still on the bench and the dirty cops were still on the beat but they had been discovered and time was running out on their careers.

The report given by Chief Swetz kept us apprised of the details behind what was found and went as follows. "As Chief of Police I am very disheartened to report that the investigation has uncovered four very dirty cops in my department. Working with the undercover FBI agents my team was able to uncover a variety of money-making schemes. I'm embarrassed and saddened that it turned out to be men I thought were my friends. It appears that they have fallen prey to one of the eternal evils, greed. A great deal of confidential information was given to these men thinking they were trusted colleagues. To make things worse it was two officers up for certain promotion within the next year. They had us all fooled given the great collars they had produced.

Unfortunately all these arrests turned out to help Big Barney and the information was given to the officers by none other than Neil "the Squeal." Both of these officers came from families that have been in law enforcement for generations.

Their fathers are both lieutenants and sadly we ascertained that they were deeply involved with their sons in these crimes. Officer Trescott and his father, Jim joined in with Big Barney first. As business expanded they recruited Officer Rhodes and his father, Mike. It was the fathers, Jim and Mike, who would find out in advance about potential raids on Big Barney's. Their sons would then pass that information on to one of Big Barney's men and collect the bribes paid for that information. Their process was quite easy, they'd pass all information on using coded napkins when visiting Big Barney's restaurant. The system netted the foursome over two hundred thousand dollars over the years. I take full responsibility. It was my managing strategy of keeping everyone informed that caused these leaks."

The judge was found by intense research into the number of times charges were dismissed, punishment was mild and associates of Big Barney were found not guilty because evidence had been lost or determined inadmissible by the judge. The evidence we found against the judge is insurmountable. He made too many blunders over the years including falsifying documents. His name is Judge Paul Petersen and was found to be living a life style far beyond his pay grade. He became trapped in this life style when his wife became accustomed to her big house and fancy jewelry. The judge's problem escalated beyond his control when his girlfriend Connie, a dancer at Big Barney's started demanding the same.

Weeks later after having a breakfast meeting with Chief Swetz I was leaving police headquarters and the dispatcher's radio screeched that shots had been fired at the courthouse. The parking lot filled with cops running and taking cover around the courthouse, which was situated right next to the police station. Bang, bang, and then a burst of Tommy gun fire ratatatat, ratatatat, ratatatatatatatat. Glass was breaking and wounded men and women were streaming from the building. "Did a criminal go raving mad inside?" I quizzed an officer who had burst out of a back door. "Heck no!" he yelled, "It's Judge Petersen. I think he's lost his mind because he's shooting at everything that moves." Then an explosion was heard coming from the back of the courthouse. We ran around the corner to find smoke everywhere. A smoke bomb had been set off probably to lay cover because you couldn't see two feet in front of yourself. Then zooooom a big Ford sedan shot by us with bullets being fired by the driver of the car. It was Judge Petersen and he was trying to escape using his own automobile. Within seconds police cars with their sirens screaming flew by us. I jumped into Chief Swetz's car and off we went in hot pursuit following a string of other police cars. Down Titus Avenue we went, each car one after the other flew into the air as it went over the first small hump heading towards Culver Road. Then crash and sparks flew as each car landed back onto the road. One officer lost control and veered off and flipped into a raspberry patch on the Alcott farm. Then we hit the big hill on Titus Avenue and given our speed had increased the distance off the road also increased as we flew over the big hill. Wow! It was like riding the Jack Rabbit at Dreamland Park and if this weren't so dangerous it would be a great thrill ride. Then we hit the first big corner and every car went around it on two wheels. Another police car spun out and landed in the yard at Titus and Culver taking out the light pole and the bus stop sign. We could see that Judge Petersen was heading down towards Big Barney's. I guessed he was looking for protection from Big Barney's crew but at the speed he was traveling he'd be very lucky if he made it that far. Up ahead was the big corner bend at Culver and Seneca Roads.

"He's not going to make that turn," shouted Chief Swetz and, sure enough, he hit a fence in the front of a small cemetery. He burst through the fence and continued into the adjacent field. He was heading for the Schum farm and the large greenhouse in their back yard. Smash, crash, he hit the greenhouse and flowers, dirt, and even chickens were tossed into the air. We all slowed down thinking that's it Judge Petersen we've got you now.

He had tried to fly the coup but instead he hit a chicken coup. Just as we started to get out of our cars and run to the greenhouse we heard a huge screech, a crash and out onto Hoffman Road burst the judge's car. He spun the tires and off he went down Hoffman and turned the corner to Wisner Road.

He shot like a bullet down Wisner Road gaining speed as he zipped past the north, center, and south entrances of Huntington Hills. He forced a car off the road, driven by George Long, but thankfully Mr. Long's car wasn't hit. He shot down the beautiful hall of trees leading into the park past the home of Johnny Currier, the guy who wrote the mystery novel, "White Lady" and veered just into the yard of Michael Abel, the rich footwear magnet and inventor of the popular Orange Crush winter boot. All of these families had children and fortunately none were out playing. As Judge Petersen tore through the park on the twisty roads he slowed down to take the last corner then shot up towards the park entrance. By this time some of the Irondequoit police had set up a roadblock to stop him. They were heavily armed and Judge Petersen would not get passed them. As Petersen approached the roadblock he increased his speed. Suddenly he swerved to try to pass between two large pine trees to avoid the roadblock. Dozens of shots rang out from all the policemen lined up behind their cars. Judge Petersen made it through the trees but many shots went through his windshield and his car spun across Culver Road and crashed into the lobby of the Hub Theater. When I arrived the police on the scene already had witnesses from inside the theater lined up. They were four boys named Arthur, Fred, Ronnie, and Roger, all armed with popcorn and pockets of marbles to roll on the floor during the movie. All were standing there examining the car that had crashed through the lobby doors. Another cute teenage couple, Gary and Teri, were just heading into the movie holding hands when Teri was hit by flying bars from the front counter. She was just fine but the officer gave her a nickel for an ice cream to calm her down. The Hub Theater staff and moviegoers were all shocked but unhurt. The children were standing with perplexed looks on their faces, all still eating their popcorn.

When Chief Swetz and I examined the scene it was obvious that the bullets through the windshield and the subsequent car crash marked the end of Judge Petersen. Apparently he heard the rumor he was about to be arrested and mistakenly thought a group of fourteen policeman entering the court were coming for him. It turned out to be a class of new recruits getting a tour of the courthouse facility. I guess Judge Petersen was feeling quite guilty and very paranoid that day. That saved the people of Irondequoit the cost of a very expensive trial. Judge Petersen would take all of his secrets to his grave. No other Big Barney conspirators were ever found in the Irondequoit court system. Judge Petersen had made a great deal of money taking bribes and he lived like a movie star. His star faded out in the lobby of the Hub Theater and then it was, fade out, roll credits, go to black, that's a wrap for the life of Judge Petersen.

As soon as Special Agent Rigoni heard about what happened he called an emergency meeting. When everyone arrived Special Agent Rigoni grabbed control of the room. "Our entire operation is in danger of discovery unless we move fast. The death of Judge Petersen is spreading like wildfire and Big Barney might get suspicious and shut down his operations until the heats off. Let's go over everything right now to see where we stand. I want all the detail. First up Sir Kuhman, can you give us an update on your investigation to date? Have you sorted out the players from the non-players and can you tell us who the top gamblers are?" "Yes sir, I have a group of seven major players, James "Jay Bird" Beale, Bill "The Ace" Richardson, Bobby "The Hatchet" Griepp, Rick "The Hot Dog" Palumbo, Jackie "Smooth" Gehers, Steve "LDR" Dimassimo and Gary "The Mark" Clarcq. These professional gamblers travel the circuit and all are exceptional players. If you're ever caught cheating any of them in a poker or dice game you'll find yourself pummeled all over your head, neck, chest and shoulders. They have been responsible for leaving cheats, braggarts and even a few big winners with broken arms, legs, noses, and a few ribs. We did not get any reports of any bodies that can be traced back to them. So we can arrest them for gambling and assault but I don't think we'll get anyone to testify against them in regards to the assaults." Agent Rigoni reacted, "I'll take anything that will place this crew behind bars. Perhaps we might entice a couple of them to turn states evidence but I doubt it! I'm sure they realize that could be a life altering event."

"Sir Kuhman, how about the alcohol shipments? Where do we stand in regards to nailing down the dealers who are making and shipping in the booze? Have you determined where it's being made and the transfer method?" "Me? No," replied Sir Kuhman. "There is great news on that front so I'll let Captain August tell you about this aspect. It was his team that exposed what we have so far."

Agent Rigoni directed his attention to me. "So, Captain August, tell us about what's been happening out on the lake." "To date Agent Rigoni, we have had no sizable shipments stopped between the port of Rochester and Canada or within two hundred miles either direction east or west on the lake. We found nothing being brought up from Irondequoit Bay, the Hojack Line, the streetcars or the roads coming up from Webster." "Where the hell is the good news in that?" asked Agent Rigoni. "Agent Rigoni, you asked for all the detail and I'm trying to tell you the progression of events. Do you want to hear it or not?" "Yes, I do," said Agent Rigoni.

"Ok then, let me continue. I decided to give a bit of a twist to your orders because it was getting a bit boring and repetitious out on the lake. Although you expressed your desire to have my crew concentrate on large ships I decided to try a different tactic and switch back to investigating small boats and ships."

"What?" shouted Agent Rigoni? "I gave you a direct order to stay away from the small crafts. Why the hell would you disobey my orders August, wasn't I clear enough? Who gave you the right to trudge off on your own? I'm running this operation. I'm in charge and I want complete control. This isn't some fly by night operation run by you Coast Watchers, damn it. I'm the FBI and I don't like losing control of any piece of this operation and I didn't want any small crafts touched. Why didn't you talk to me before you ran off half-assed?"

Now the room fell completely silent as tempers started to get out of control. I tried to continue with my report and keep a level of professionalism but I was on the edge and my emotions were about to spill out.

"Agent Rigoni, hold on to your britches, you need to get the entire picture. As I was saying, it seemed like we were wasting our time far out on the lake because I was finding nothing. Sir Kuhman's men were seeing truck after truck coming in and out of Big Barney's but none of the deliveries seemed to be booze. Besides, my men were exhausted from constant duty day and night. We had seen absolutely nothing of interest and our inspections found a few illegal fishing trawlers but nothing else for weeks on end. Therefore I decided to shut down that part of the lake operation for just one week. I was certain that another tactic was necessary if we were to produce any real results. So I sent some teams off on reconnaissance fishing trips to relax and watch for traffic patterns on the lake."

Once again Agent Rigoni jumped up and with his face beet red and yelled, "You must be an idiot or just incompetent at your job!" Now I had hit my boiling point, so I stepped over to Agent Rigoni and stood nose to nose with him my emotions burst. "Who the hell do you think you are talking to some rookie? Before I continue with my report let me remind you Agent Rigoni that I don't really work for you. We are partners in this effort. I do not take orders from you that I will blindly follow like a robot. I also want you to know that you have crossed a line that you only want to cross once with me. You had best mind your tone, sir. I'm a very tired man and my crew and I have given our all to this team. So I'm putting you on notice right now. If you don't start treating me with a modicum of respect there is going to be some immediate reckoning. You keep on this path and you'll find yourself sidelined for the duration into Rochester's Northside Hospital broken bone repair unit. You don't want to insult me, my men, or any one of us Coast Watchers, got it?"

Agent Rigoni looked like his eyes were about to shoot lightning bolts and steam was about to come out of his ears. "WHAT DID YOU SAY TO ME?" he shrieked. Sir Kuhman stepped between us, and with a calm voice said, "Gentlemen, we're all exhausted. Let's think about the mission and let this go for now. We'll put the boxing gloves on after Big Barney's in prison." "All right for now," Agent Rigoni replied in a more civil voice. But fishing, he told his men to go fishing." Agent Rigoni's voice shot up again and he bellowed, "Have you lost your mind August?" At this point I had been redlined by this guy and was getting out of control and I shouted back, "No I'm not going crazy, but you're about to lose some teeth." Sir Kuhman stepped in again and in a very harsh tone insisted, "Shut your mouth and listen Rigoni or you'll be tangling with both of us. Your entire attitude is making me wonder where your head's at man. Let the man finish his report and then you can talk. But for now sit your ass down."

At that point Agent Rigoni decided he'd better sit down and listen. I continued, "As I was saying, I sent some of my crew on reconnaissance fishing trips. I sent two to Henderson Harbor, two to Alexandria Bay, and two as far up as Massena. After a few days I started thinking I might have made an error but then I received a report back from Seaman Mike Allen and Seaman Robert Karl assigned to Henderson Harbor. They noticed a 24-foot Chris Craft going in and out from shore at what seemed to be frequent intervals. Then they saw a few camping trailers leaving from the same area where the Chris Craft visited every day, so they decided to investigate. Sure enough that was it, they were certain they found the source of a major bootlegger.

After a few more days of investigation Seamen Allen and Karl were able to plot the entire path of the operation. It was actually quite ingenious and after further investigation the trail led directly back towards Canada and a small Island named Main Duck Island. Main Duck Island is just over the border and this little spot on the lake turned out to be a huge staging area for many distilleries from Canada. The two seamen found various small crafts delivering booze to Main Duck Island from many points in mainland Canada. After that, the booze was moved by ship past Galloo Island to the interior of Stony Island where there's a small lake that gives the bootleggers exceptional shelter from storms. Another great feature of Stony Island is that for the most part it's not inhabited so the shippers can come and go with anonymity. From that point the booze was moved to a pond in an area along Route 3 known as Ramsey Shore. They'd drive their ships into a small pond right past the summer home of the famous landscape painter Donald Bigelow. Mr. Bigelow and his German girlfriend, Fraulein Vidahoffer, travel the world to high-class art shows and therefore are rarely home. The shipper's destination however was a cottage that we discovered to be owned by the notorious Sally Salzman, lawyer, and bookmaker, from the east side of Manhattan. The next move was easy. They'd transfer the booze into camping trailers parked in an area called Elsie's Field adjacent to Salzman's. Later we learned that the trailers had been hollowed out and could store a great deal of inventory. The trailers had vacation stickers from the Willows, Yellowstone Park, Mt. Rushmore, Miami Beach, etc. splattered all over the rear of each trailer. I assumed this was done to make them look like an average family camper heading on vacation."

"The next step was the toughest yet most important part of this operation, delivering the goods to Big Barney's. After we were sure we had the delivery route to Ramsey Shore nailed we decided to watch the trailers leave and follow them. Thinking they would head for another warehouse operation we followed them all the way to Rochester. To our surprise they went directly to Big Barney's. So we hung in, waited and watched diligently. The driver parked in the back of Big Barney's parking lot reserved for cars with boats and camping trailers. The driver got out of his car, never opened his trailer and went straight into the restaurant. He sat down near the band to have dinner and listen to music. After an hour or so he came back out and got into the back seat of his car and went to sleep. We kept a close watch on the trailer and the car all night and saw nothing. The next morning the driver got back into the front seat and drove off. We followed close behind and he drove right back to Ramsey Shore. It was easy to see that the trailer was riding much higher and bouncing more so we knew it was empty but we had no idea how or when they emptied it. We were mystified!"

"So what the hell did you learn?" demanded Agent Rigoni. "We learned that he parked the trailer hooked up to another trailer and within a few hours he headed right back to Big Barney's. At a gas stop we pulled in on the opposite side of the pump and when he went in to pay we were able to see that this trailer was full." "So what do we have here?" asked Agent Rigoni. "A man who loves Big Barney's food and can make booze disappear?" "No sir, a mystery solved by my men and a tunnel that leads from Big Barney's basement to the back parking lot and comes up right under the center of the camping trailer. The trailer comes in full and leaves empty and no one sees the offload because it's done at night and from under the delivery trailer."

"Okay, good work, Captain August. "Please send on my congratulations to Seaman Karl and Allen." "You mean Third Class Petty Officers Karl and Allen. Captain August has promoted them, a jolly good show and well deserved," said Sir

Kuhman. "So we've got them all and we can wrap this up today," stated Agent Rigoni. "Well, no sir," I replied. "There is something bothering me and I need a few days and the help of your undercover agents." "Are you crazy? We have to close in right away and shut this operation down permanently," replied Agent Rigoni.

"Why are you in such a hurry, Rigoni?" I was starting to lose my temper again so I took a deep breath and continued. "Agent Rigoni, I believe you're jumping the gun on this. It seems that you are willing to settle for sweeping Big Barney and his men into a cell for a few years. But how much do we really have on them? Even if we catch them with dice in their hands, cards in their pockets while sipping a martini, is gambling and booze enough to get them sent to prison for life? The answer is NO! Big Barney will get out in three or four years and start all over again in a different city. Hell, Neil "the Squeal" and Felton "the Fiend" will most likely be out in a year, two at the most, and to me that's not good enough. Don't we want these guys to hang for their crimes, including the murders we all know in our hearts they've committed? Those monsters have piled up a stack of bodies under the direction of Big Barney and I want to find the evidence to prove it." Agent Rigoni protested but Chief Swetz and Sir Kuhman agreed with me that the risk, if successful, far outweighed what we might lose in evidence if Big Barney shuts his operation down before we get to close in. "We can arrest them for gambling anytime. Besides, if they shut down and then vanished, the affect will be the same to this community."

"Agent Rigoni, I for one would like to hear Captain August's plan. After that we can all appraise whether it has merit," said Sir Kuhman. "Okay, Captain August what have you got in mind?" Agent Rigoni added with a sarcastic tone. "Well sir, one of my men came to me with a sticker off of a broken bottle he found in a fire pit at Ramsey Shore. The label had a horse riding a lightning bolt. That sticker was the same logo as the ones I saw on bottles ten years ago when we stopped a yacht named "Dill" about 25 miles out on the lake. The subsequent search of that yacht resulted in finding that the men on board murdered the yachts true owner Peter Pundt the pickle manufacturer. We later found out that cronies of the guys we caught had most likely been responsible for murdering his family. We never found the killers of his wife and children but I feel we have a real chance of finding them now if my hunch turns out to be right. I have already put out some feelers and we got some information from the FBI Agents 0008 and 00LX planted in Big Barney's operation. According to them they are 90% sure that Big Barney owns the distillery that uses that label. Agent V thinks he even knows who the main contact is at Big Barney's Distillery. After all, Big Barney must have a plant manager and Agent 0008 thinks he knows just who that manager is. If you give me two days, three at the most I think we can solve those murders and I believe all will lead back to Big Barney."

"Okay," agreed Special Agent Rigoni. "I don't like waiting and you'll take full responsibility for this change of plans. I'm not too optimistic but I'll give you three days max and then we're moving in. If we hear from our undercover agents or see any sign that Big Barney is planning to shut down and disappear we will move immediately with or without you August. Agreed?" "Agreed," I responded.

Sir Kuhman was the next to talk. "Captain August, I'll have all my team drop what they're doing and help. If we combine forces perhaps we can increase the odds of success." "Great idea," said Chief Swetz. "My men are also at your disposal, let's get this done." "Okay, I'm going to need an airplane. Can anyone get access to a plane and a good pilot?" Sir Kuhman stood up and said, "You can use my plane." "You have your own plane?" I asked. "Of course Captain August, at Scotland Yard we all had our own planes, don't you? Also, I'm the best pilot I know. Well, at least the best in this room." "Sir Kuhman, can you take orders from a measly captain?" I asked. "It will be an honor sir," he replied. I then gathered all the key players around me and showed them my plan.

"Gentlemen, we received word from Agents 0008 and 00LX that the manager of Big Barney's distillery comes in from Canada every other day by boat. They think he's a Canadian citizen because he has the habit of saying "eh" at the end of almost every sentence. Agent 00LX said he'd get word to us the next time he shows up to meet with Big Barney. Now that we have a description of the guy we'll keep him under constant surveillance after he leaves Big Barney's so we can find that distillery. Next, we need to find out if the distillery uses a bottle label that looks like a horse riding a lightning bolt. If they do, we need to capture the distillery manager and interrogate him and his crew to see if they know anything about the Peter Pundt murders. Chief Swetz is an expert at interrogation and he'll sweat the hell out of them. If they have information and we can connect Big Barney to these murders, we'll capture Big Barney, then try him and fry him. Otherwise, we'll have to settle on the charges we can prove." "No hanging from the yardarm Captain," commented Sir Kuhman. "Hanging, electric chair, firing squad, anything that results in a burial is okay with me," I replied.

The decision was made to hop on Sir Kuhman's plane to see if we could spot Big Barney's distillery manager coming in from Canada. Sir Kuhman, Petty Officer Allen, and I took off to search for any boat making the crossing from Canada to the U.S.A. We hadn't spotted anything of interest and we were almost all the way across the lake when Petty Officer Allen happened to spot a speedboat pulling out of a small harbor. Back behind the speedboat was a building with a smokestack that had a great deal of smoke or steam coming out of it. The speedboat Allen spotted was headed straight out at full throttle. Sir Kuhman said to Petty Officer Allen, "Could it be this easy? Is it possible that we found what we're looking for just by tripping on it? Let's keep looking along the coast. We'll catch up with that speedboat later. If he's heading for the states he's got a long ride and he'll be on the lake for hours. Let's head up the coast, perhaps I'll find a nice fishing spot to relax at when I take my next holiday," Sir Kuhman joked.

After seeing a couple potential locations to investigate Sir Kuhman said that our fuel was getting low so we'd better head back. Off we went and started to search for the speedboat we saw earlier leaving that small harbor. It was only about 45 minutes and we spotted it again and sure enough it was making a beeline direct to the Port of Rochester.

The lake was calm and flat and you could spot the speedboat's wake long before you could see the speedboat itself. There were a few puffy clouds, a bright blue sky and the lake looked deep blue. I could see the Rochester Airport off in the distance and the men in the tower called us right in.

As soon as we landed I contacted Chief Swetz and requested he assign some men to look for a white speedboat that should be coming into the harbor within an hour or so. "If it arrives have surveillance ready to see if it has a guy on board that fits the description of Big Barney's distillery manager. Then please report back to me immediately. Chief, please confirm that this is the guy but don't let him know he's being watched, just confirm his identity. I'll wait at the phone for your response."

Sir Kuhman, "If it's the manager on board we need to take off and head right back to Canada. We need to check out the building with the smokestacks. It's essential that we determine if booze is being manufactured in that building. If so, does their label have a horse riding a lightning bolt?"

We had an hour or two to wait so I said to Sir Kuhman, "How about taking a bit of time for a quick lunch? I know my men and I are starved, how about you?" "I could eat one of the Queen's stallions," Sir Kuhman replied. So I sent my crew out on a road trip to my favorite local hot dog stand, LDR's, in Charlotte. Yah, it was a bit of a drive but the food is worth waiting for. They returned with hot dogs, hamburgers, steak sandwiches, french-fries, onion rings and chocolate milkshakes. The meal was over the moon great and we stuffed ourselves. A short time later after having lunch I received the call. "Yes, that's Big Barney's guy all right," "Okay Chief Swetz, if he tries to leave and go back to Canada, detain him for whatever reason you can come up with." "That'll be easy Captain, he has the worst looking suit I've ever seen and that alone should get him arrested for indecency," he chuckled.

So, Sir Kuhman, Petty Officer Allen, and I got back on the refueled plane and took off again. Sir Kuhman tried to make the flight back to Canada comfortable. He said, "Relax guys, take a nap. We'll be up here for a bit. I'll wake you when we get near the coast of Canada." After reclining his seat Petty Officer Allen suddenly popped back up. "Oh no, Sir Kuhman, did we get authorization to fly back and forth between the U.S.A. and Canada?" "You bet," Sir Kuhman responded, "We're all set, I secured the rights to do so hours ago. I have many friends in the Canadian Mounties and they gave me the go-ahead. Canadas part of England after all and they don't like bootleggers in Canada any more than they do in the United States. They're not taxpayers and they add to the criminal activity in Canada. So we're all set. If we land I'll be stretching it so we'll have to leave quickly. Then it will be too late for them to object to us anyway. If they call to protest, have them talk to Agent Rigoni, let him handle it. That will give him more to complain about. Anyway, I haven't figured out yet why Agent Rigoni is being so intolerant, and that puzzles me, something odd is afoot. Is he afraid he won't capture the headlines on this one?"

Within a short time we were approaching our destination. "We need to find a place to set the plane down. A field or a good country road without traffic will do the trick," said Sir Kuhman. We spotted a great place to set down but we'd have to get in and out quickly well before dusk. We landed on a gravel road and parked the plane just off the edge in a field. Sir Kuhman turned the plane around so it pointed back down the road ready for taking off again. We all headed across the field to check out the distillery. As we approached we noticed a huge trash bin so we thought we'd start there. Petty Officer Allen volunteered to climb in to see what it held. As soon as he traversed the top edge he slipped and slid straight to the bottom inside. We heard a big splash and then from Allen, "DANG. YUCK." It had rained the day before and the bin had a great deal of water in it. Seconds later Petty Officer Allen climbed out with a bunch of labels with a horse riding a lightning bolt. They were on the end of a roll used in a packing operation. That clinched it, this was the place where Big Barney was manufacturing booze and the label linked this place to the Peter Pundt murders. Not proof enough to make any arrest but we just took a giant leap forward.

Unfortunately, Allen also climbed out covered in moldy french fries, rotten coleslaw, horseradish, and decaying squishy fish. It was on him from head to toe including his face and he was drenched with water that reeked. I had never smelled anything so putrid in my life and it was dripping from him. Then there was a shout from the building, "Hey, who's out there?" With that we all started moving as quietly and as fast as we could toward the plane. "We should have left you behind Sir Kuhman to keep the plane running and ready to go." "Don't worry about that, just get to the plane as fast as your legs will carry you." Soon we were all there and as we approached we started to hear barking dogs and then a couple of shots. "Holy smoke they're shooting at us!" Allen yelled. Then Sir Kuhman dropped to the ground just as we heard the boom of a shotgun. "Are you hit," asked Petty Officer Allen as he stopped to help Sir Kuhman up. "Yes, I'll be all right. They hit me in my posterior and it stings like hell. Let's get into the plane and we'll figure it out after we take off."

We got to the plane and Sir Kuhman got it started and off we went. "Get out the flashlight and look to see how serious the wound is," shouted Sir Kuhman. He was in obvious pain but I couldn't find a bullet hole or blood. "You're in a better position to see Allen, so here's the flashlight. Pull his pants down further so we can get a better look at how bad he's hit." As soon as Allen pulled Sir Kuhman's pants down he started to laugh. "You'll be fine sir I've seen this before when I was 12 years old. You've been hit in the butt and legs with rock salt. It's going to sting like a thousand bees and burn like thunder, but you'll live. Now you know what it feels like to get caught snitching apples and get shot in the butt because you didn't get over the fence fast enough."

Now that we were in the clear and we knew that our pilot would be able to fly us home another problem hit us all like a ton of bricks. "Petty Office Allen, YOU STINK and it's worse than the pain in my butt. Oh my God, I think I'll have to crash the plane or make you get out," yelled Sir Kuhman. "Get out, what do you mean get out, get out to where?" said Allen. "Out into the lake, how long can you tread water Allen? You are making my eyes sting," cried Sir Kuhman. So the windows came down the heat was turned up and all you could hear was cantankerous grumbling in the compartment all the way back across the lake.

When we landed they must have thought the plane was on fire because we stopped far out on the runway and jumped out. The men in the control tower saw it and sent the fire engine and as soon as they arrived Sir Kuhman yelled, "SPRAY HIM, HE STINKS!" As the word spread and everyone realized why we stopped so far out firemen gathered and started tossing soap and sponges. A fireman's jumpsuit was also offered to allow Petty Office Allen to change into clean clothes right on the runway. "Standing out here in the buff with all of us looking on is a bit humbling isn't it Allen?" Sir Kuhman joked. The fireman continued to spray Petty Officer Allen as Sir Kuhman and I trotted over to grab a ride back to the hanger to contact Chief Swetz and Agent Rigoni. As we jogged down the runway I shouted back, "Petty Officer Allen, you have the rest of the night off to soak in a highly scented bubble bath, and that's an order."

"The time has arrived to start putting the lid on Big Barney's operation," I shouted. "Sir Kuhman, I'll call Chief Swetz and you call Agent Rigoni to pull together as many members of the team as possible for a late night meeting." When Sir Kuhman and I arrived at the main terminal we each grabbed a phone and started to make calls. We then headed to our operation center. As soon as we were all gathered I stood up on the center table and declared enthusiastically, "We have the link to the murders of Peter Pundt's family." The room erupted with joy knowing that all of our hard work might now lead to a murder conviction for Big Barney and his brothers. "Now all we need to do is hope one of the guys who came across the lake tonight on that speedboat knows about those murders and is willing to make a deal and turn on Big Barney. I can feel it in my bones Big Barney is complicit in these murders. Chief Swetz, please apprehend every person who gets on that speedboat in the morning. Call me at my home as soon as that happens no matter what time."

Sir Kuhman and I went off to get some shut-eye. At 5:30am I heard a ringing. I sprang up, grabbed the phone and said, "Captain August here." Then I realized there was no one on the phone, it was my doorbell. I rushed to the door and outside stood two police officers Doug Reid Green and Gloria Kins. "The chief wants you at headquarters right away. This morning we nabbed Big Barney's men from Canada getting on their boat. They had four satchels full of cash and orders to replenish Big Barney's inventory. We caught them red handed with all the proof we need to jail these boys for years and years." "All RIGHT!" I exclaimed. "Now we just need to find out if one of them is ready to sing."

When I got to the police station Chief Swetz had already started to interview the top guy. It turned out his name was Leonardo Grape and the chief was right, he was wearing the most ridiculous suit. Chief Swetz was an expert at interrogation and Grape was already sweating bullets. According to Grape he didn't know anything outside of the distillery operation and this seemed plausible because he had only joined Big Barney's team about seven years ago. "Please, I have a family and they depend on me," whimpered Grape. "Okay, I can make your stay at Attica more comfortable and a bit shorter if you can give us a good answer to this question. Out of the two men who were arrested with you which one has been with Big Barney the longest?" "That's easy," said Grape, "Larry has been with Big Barney since the beginning. Larry Richards, he knows everything about Big Barney's operation, talk to Larry." "Bring me Richards NOW!" shouted Chief Swetz.

In the door came Richards, a great big guy with tattoos, a Fu Man Chu mustache and a bald head. He had a smug grin on his face and he was missing teeth in the front. This was one mean looking thug. Chief Swetz started in on him, "Richards, I have a few questions to ask you. If you give me any static let me assure you that you are looking at a jail sentence that will amount to years in prison. The hardest time you can ever imagine. I will make sure they put you in with guys that eat guys like you for lunch. We have many open bunks with guys that have some serious psychological issues and love to have new blood to abuse in their cells. Perhaps one of them will make you their new sweetheart. They're always looking for a handsome guy like you. You know the type I'm talking about, don't you Richards? You can make life easier for yourself and reduce your time if you're willing to cooperate. You better put your brain in gear. I need the answer to some questions, right now."

Suddenly this mean looking thug burst into tears and sobbed like a baby. He gave in faster than Grape. "I'll tell you anything you want just don't toss me in with those nuts I can't take being beat up." "Okay Richards, here's what we need and I need it right now or I'll be sure to personally introduce you to your new cell buddy, got it Richards?" "Yes sir, I'll help you if I can, what do you want?" "I want you to think back ten years ago to the day a group of pirates grabbed a yacht called the "Dill". They murdered the owner and his family and I'm sure these scumbags were from Big Barney's distillery in Canada. I want to know who these guys were and then I want to hang them for what they did. Now tell me Richards do you remember these murders? The ship was named "Dill" and the story hit the front page of every newspaper between Buffalo and Montreal."

Richards eyes lit up, "Is that it? Is that all you want? I give you the names and you'll talk to the district attorney to help me with my sentence, right?" "Yes," said Chief Swetz. "But if you lie I'll personally make sure you'll..." "No, no, no," interrupted Richards. "I hate the guys who did that and I'm glad to tell you all I know." "Are you willing to testify in court if needed?" said Chief Swetz. "Yes sir, if you fellas protect me from Big Barney and his gang," said Richards. "I'll protect you from Big Barney. I promise. Now let's hear it Richards, start talking."

Richards started to tell his account. He had us hanging on every word. "I remember the day like it was yesterday. Big Barney and his brothers, Neil "the Squeal" and Felton "the Fiend", came across the lake to look over the distilling operation. A guy named Hetko was with them and a few other wise guys. This Hetko was a real bad guy. He scared the hell out of me and I'm not easy to scare, at least I wasn't back then. I remember Big Barney was in a good mood and he tripped one guy and pushed him off the dock into the freezing cold lake. That day sticks in my mind like glue because the guy he pushed was me. It's also the day when I really started to hate Big Barney and all his brothers with great intensity. Neil "the Squeal" offered his hand to help me up from the water but just before I was on the dock he let go and pushed me back in. Neil and that big jerk Felton "the Fiend" were laughing at me so hard Felton almost fell in himself. I was scared to death of those wise guys. I wouldn't put it passed them to shoot me if I got mad so I just laughed it off and went home to change my clothes. I don't live too far away, right down Buescher Road. When I got back from changing they were gone. I didn't see them leave so I don't know exactly who went out with Big Barney or how much of a load they took but I think two or three of Hetko's thugs left with them. I recognized a few of the goons. Their names were Billitier, Heym, Morrow and a new guy they called German. As I said I don't know who went back out with Big Barney, but this group of creeps were the only men around. The distillery was closed that day. I was the watchman then so I know for sure who could have gone out with Big Barney, but I don't know who actually did."

"Is that all you have," said Chief Swetz? "Oh no, not at all, that's only the beginning, what happened later that afternoon was odd and scary. I saw Big Barney's ship coming back in towards the dock. I remember thinking to myself I'm at the wrong place at the wrong time because when I spotted Big Barney he was very unhappy. I could see an extremely menacing look on Big Barney's face before the ship was even near the dock."

Richards face became somber and he seemed remorseful. "You know guys, with my body and a mug like this I've had to spend my life acting like a big tough guy. I've never committed any bad crimes beyond hauling booze. I'd rather just farm if I could make a living at it. I hope you guys don't think I'm scum like Big Barney." At that point Richards began to sob. "Go on Richards, get it all on the table," Chief Swetz said with a very empathetic tone. But Richards looked at one of the officers in the room and said, "Hey copper, can you get me a cup of coffee and a peanut butter and jelly sandwich? I'm getting real hungry here." Chief Swetz gave an affirming nod to his man so the officer said, "Sure, do you want butter on it also?" "NO, for goodness sakes, who would put butter on a peanut butter and jelly sandwich? Yikes that would taste awful." Richards then stuck his thumb up in a backwards motion towards the officer and said to Chief Swetz, "Your officer Kenny doesn't even know how to make a P and J sandwich. Do you trust him with a gun?" The room broke up in laughter.

"Let's keep going Richards. You can have a jar of peanut butter and jelly and a whole loaf of bread, whatever you want for dinner after we're done here," said Chief Swetz. Richards went on with his story. "Okay now where'd I leave off? Oh yah, Big Barney was coming into shore at what seemed like a very high rate of speed, I thought he might not stop in time and hit the dock hard but he managed to stop. Big Barney yelled to me," "Hey you Richards, yah you, do you want to live past morning or do you want your life to end right here and now?" "Now I want to tell you guys, he wasn't kidding, any good mood Big Barney had when he left in the morning was gone and he was irate, nervous, maybe panicked or something. Big Barney was in a great rush and his brothers had the same hurried and nasty looks on their faces. I was shaking in my boots, I'll tell you. I was certain there were many more guys who went out on the ship and yet only three returned. I had the only car there and everyone was gone when I got back from changing my wet clothes and that great big guy Hetko didn't walk away. I thought they had a gun battle and Big Barney and his brothers were the only ones that lived through it. Possibly Big Barney decided to reduce the number of employees he had and do it the simple way, shoot them. My fear was starting to go beyond petrified, where were the others I wondered?

A few seconds passed and Big Barney was right in front of me and he grabbed my shirt pulled me right to his face and said, "Did you hear me boy?" "Do you want to live or are you prepared to die right now?" At that point I was real quick to respond. "Oh yah, I want to live Big Barney. What do you need Big Barney, anything you want, anything sir." "Now you're thinking boy," said Big Barney. "I want you to gather every spent shell in the base of that ship, the Tommy gun and anything else you find on the floor, and put it all into this burlap sack. Then I want you to clean out that ship until it is so sparkling clean you can eat off the floor, GOT IT!" "Yes sir," I said. "I've got it, real clear Big Barney." "I want you to make sure the rags, the sponge, everything you use to cleanup are placed into this burlap sack. Then put in some heavy rocks, tie the bag with bailing wire and go as far out as you can in that small motor boat the one right next to mine and dump it all into the lake." "Do you have that or do I need to repeat it." "I got it Big Barney, clean it all up and make sure the shells, the gun, the rags, everything including a few rocks go in that bag and toss it all in far out in the lake. Come back only with a very empty boat and make sure your ship shines like a baby's butt and is so clean you can eat off the floor. I got it Big

Barney, I got it". "One more thing," said Big Barney, "Give me your car keys. I need to take your car for a ride. I'll return it in the morning when I come to check and make sure that you completed all my requests. If you don't..." "NO NEED TO SAY BIG BARNEY. It will be done and done perfectly." Then Big Barney left. He had my car returned to me the next night. He never did come back and I never saw him at the distillery again, ever. It was not long after that he put Leonardo Grape in charge and Big Barney stayed in the USA. The day after all this happened I saw the newspaper headlines that the Pickle King was killed. I figured that Big Barney was connected in some way. I knew it couldn't be a coincidence that I found monogramed towels and a jar of Pickles all with the Pickle King's logo on them in the ship I had just cleaned to a spit shine.

"All right Richards, that helped a great deal now eat your sandwich," said Chief Swetz. "Agent Rigoni, will his testimony help us put Big Barney away or better yet get him hung?" Sir Kuhman interrupted and said, "What if by some miracle we could find all that stuff Richards dumped? If he could narrow down the area for us and we sent divers in to find the gun and shells then we'd have a much better chance of hanging Big Barney, right Chief?" "It would sure go a long way in verifying Richards's story. But the odds of finding it all are long and any finger print evidence will be gone for sure after being in the lake for ten years," said Chief Swetz. Then Richards bounced in and said "If I help you find this stuff can you arrange for my sentence to be parole only, no jail? My only crime is delivering booze and being a watchman, I never hurt anyone." "Yah sure kid," said Chief Swetz. "However, as I mentioned before finding that stuff at the bottom of the lake is a very, very long shot. It also depends on how far out you dumped the stuff because our divers can only go so deep. Richards, do you have any idea how far you out on the lake were when you dumped that stuff?" "Sure I do, as far out as the upper loft of my barn. I never dumped the stuff in the lake Chief." "WHAT?" said Chief Swetz, "You heard me right Chief I never dumped it," said Richards. "I wasn't going to throw away a perfectly good Tommy gun. Hell Big Barney and his brothers even left a belt of ammo and a full jar and a half of Peter Pundt Pickles." "DO YOU MEAN YOU STILL HAVE THE GUN?" asked Chief Swetz. "Sure, I still have all of the stuff I found in Big Barney's ship, bullet casings, bloody rags, the jar and a half of pickles, the monogrammed towels and the Tommy gun. I put it all in the potato sack just like Big Barney ordered me to do. After I cleaned the ship I got to thinking about the money I could get for the Tommy gun. I just couldn't bring myself to dump it and after all Big Barney was long gone. I figured Big Barney would get killed someday given the business he was in and then I'd sell the Tommy. So I grabbed the sack and ran home to hide it. I'm not a rich guy like you fellas and those Tommy's are worth hundreds of dollars. That's a lot of bread man, perhaps I could get as much as $300 then I could buy one of those new Ford Model T's."

"After I got the stuff stashed away in my barn I never even looked at it again. I've thought many times of throwing it all away but I was too afraid to even take it out of the barn to do that. It would be my luck I'd pull it out of its hiding place and Big Barney would show up as I was walking it to my car. Therefore, it sits untouched right where I originally put it ten years ago."

At this juncture the entire room erupted and Richards started getting pats on his back. Everyone on the team was elated with the exception of Agent Rigoni. He just kept a stern look on his face. "Okay men, we have all we need now. All we have to do is go to Canada and get the evidence before we go to trial. With the testimony of Richards and all the evidence we've gathered we have cornered Big Barney and his brothers. It's time to make our next stop BIG Barney's!" yelled Chief Swetz.

About an hour after the meeting broke up I went home to get a few hours of shut-eye. The meeting went into the wee hours of the morning and we had eyes and ears on Big Barney. Our plan was to hit Big Barney's place at 11:00pm that night. Agent Rigoni requested he be given four or five hours to warn his undercover agents. However, the main reason we set the hour so late was because Chief Swetz insisted a late start. He was very concerned for the safety of the neighborhood children. It was October 31, Halloween, and there would be too many children out on the streets in the early evening hours. The time was finally set. It had been months but the day of reckoning had come for Big Barney. It would be particularly crowded at Big Barney's because it was Halloween. He always held a huge Halloween party for the adults.

The day went by exceptionally fast, probably because I slept through most of it. Agent Rigoni and Chief Swetz had everything in place and we had hundreds of men ready. Most of the officers would be covering the entrances and exits and our plan was to corral everyone in the parking area as the gamblers and restaurant customers streamed out. The back of Big Barney's had no windows and no doors but we covered it anyway with one officer, just in case. We also blocked off the key streets that would have kids in costumes running around. We employed an old tactic of having a fake sewer repair crew just to keep any kids away who might still be out that late. I decided to stay home until 7:00pm because I knew the night would be long and we had everything ready to roll. I was asleep on my couch when at about 5:30 there was a bang on my door. I sprang up and ran to find out who was there. My concern, did something go wrong, did Chief Swetz send someone to get me? I rushed onto my porch so fast I scarred the heck out of the children standing on my steps.

My mind was still in a fog when I opened the door and immediately came out of it as soon as the night air hit my body. "Trick or Treat" the children yelled. Oh yah, it's Halloween. My thoughts were bouncing back and forth as I served treats to the children. I started to think about

Halloween night at Big Barney Sahs Restaurant. I don't believe in ghosts but I do have to admit that Big Barneys was a very strange place to be on Halloween night. Something about that place gives me the creeps especially on Halloween night. There was always a huge rise in calls from Big Barney's to the Police and Fire Departments. On Halloween night last year there were fires in the kitchen. Three people claimed that someone tripped them on the staircase, yet no one ever saw who had done it. Most of all so many people said they saw ghosts of slaves in chains, firemen all bandaged up from being burned, old drunks stumbling around, the former Sea Breeze Fire Chief yelling orders and soldiers in a variety of civil war and revolutionary war uniforms just leaning against the walls and holding each other up. The saddest report was that one soldier was sitting, crying and asking for his mama.

Looking out to my yard I saw trudging through the leaves a band of trick-or-treaters laughing and giggling. This group of children ran up to the house and I recognized their faces. "Let's see who do we have here? I see Lexi, Trevor, Gabrielle, Livia, and who's this little guy in the police outfit?" "That's Noah," said Lexi I gave them their treat and they were off and running. In seconds another group ran up to take their place. I dropped the treats into their bag and they were gone like the wind.

As they ran away I noticed that it looked like a rainstorm was moving in. Our operation would start in just over five hours and I hoped that the rain would hold off until way past midnight. As I dropped candy into the bags of the next group of little goblins my telephone rang and I stopped to answer it.

It was Chief Swetz and he wanted me to come to headquarters right away. So I put the rest of the candy in a bowl with a sign to please take only one. I set the bowl outside the front door, locked up, and sped off to police headquarters on Titus Ave. When I got to the station Sir Kuhman was also pulling in behind me along with many others. Everyone was heading for the door of the chief's office. As soon as all the key players were there Chief Swetz came in and said, "We are moving up the time, we need to hit them right now! I got word from one of Agent Rigoni's inside men that Big Barney is getting real nervous or someone has tipped him off. He's been acting stranger than usual. One of the agents saw him packing his car with food, clothing, and a case that had a heavy lock that he chained to the floor of the car. I'm afraid he might be planning to disappear at least until the heats off. So we'll have to hit them RIGHT NOW." Agent Rigoni, have you warned your men?" "Yes, I have. They're expecting us later tonight but they'll adjust as they see things going down. "That's great," said Chief Swetz. "Before we head out I'd like to get a team of volunteer's to apprehend our crooked cops, the Trescott and Rhodes father and son teams. Tell them I want them to report immediately for a highly classified meeting. As soon as they enter the building and surrender their guns to the weapons locker clerk, have your team arrest them. I don't want to give them any chance of escaping or using their guns. As soon as you have them in handcuffs place them in a nice cell at our headquarters retention center. They should start getting used to prison life and there is no time like the present. Do I have any volunteers?" The Marsala brothers, Captain Steve Marsala, Sergeant Lou Marsala and also Lieutenant Russell Rex all stepped forward. Captain Marsala said, "Chief, my brother and I went to the Academy with both Trescott and Rhodes and Lieutenant Rex worked with their fathers for years. This will go down much easier if we pick them up. We've had to do that in the past for special ops so they won't suspect anything. I think the three of us can handle this easily." "Magnificent idea, Go," said Chief Swetz. "Now for the rest, let's head out. Remember your training. Let's all get back here safe and sound," yelled Chief Swetz.

The time had finally come and we were surrounding Big Barney's. The operation would be run by Chief Swetz because he was in charge of local law enforcement. The Chief was busy giving last minute instructions to the leader of the assault team, Lieutenant Mendoza. How strange that on this night of all nights, Halloween, we will catch a monster that has been haunting Rochester and the town of Irondequoit for years. It seems almost a cliché that it should all culminate on Halloween night, cliché but very appropriate. I prayed that all would go well and the men and women on our force would remain safe. Sir Kuhman leaned over to me and said, "I don't see any of Big Barney's men hanging around the veranda at the front door. I think he's been tipped off so we need to be extra vigilant."

The words of caution had no sooner left the lips of Sir Kuhman when we heard a sharp "crack". A rifle shot rang out from one of the upper windows and the front windshield of a police wagon was shattered just above where Agent Rigoni was standing. Then, bang, bang, bang, too many shots to count coming from Big Barney's. We had been noticed and Big Barney's men opened up on us. Chief Swetz yelled, "Plan B, plan B, GO!" Chief Swetz prepared alternate assault strategies to try to anticipate in advance what might happen when we arrived at Big Barney's. Plan B was devised just in case our operation was detected. We had hoped to get the drop on them and find Big Barney's crew unprepared, but that was not to be. The next thing I heard was the sound of tear gas grenades being shot into the windows of Big Barney's. It was then that all hell broke loose. Police Lieutenant G. F. Mendoza and his assault team went into motion and after shooting the tear gas grenades Chris's team used a battering ram to break through the double doors leading into the rear of the building. As the door burst open, two of Big Barney's crew holding Tommy guns opened fire on the assault team. Lieutenant Mendoza immediately neutralized one of them with a burst from his gun but then spun around and was thrown back against the wall. He was hit. The second man stopped firing and turned to retreat back into Big Barney's. He didn't get two steps when men from the assault team neutralized him with a burst of fire from most of the members of the assault team. Possible injuries had been anticipated and medics were at the ready. Seconds after Lieutenant Mendoza was hit Officers Nicky and Adele, two highly trained Coast Guard medics, whisked him to safety with a severe gunshot wound to his shoulder. The scene was chaotic, patrons were rushing out doors and climbing out windows trying to escape the tear gas or find cover from the bullets coming from Big Barney's men. Agents were bursting through every door and gunshots rang out from all over the building. Chief Swetz assigned one team to keep an eye on the secret passage used by the camping trailers to deliver goods. Men and women were attempting escape from there but they were being rounded up as fast as they came out of the hole. I followed Sir Kuhman in the side door and he was immediately shot in the arm. He raised his gun and took out that thug with a volley of shots. Sir Kuhman said, "That chap shot the wrong arm. He left my gun hand untouched, his misfortune." As I was helping Sir Kuhman up I realized that we were completely exposed from the rear. As I peeked back a goon came rushing out of the pantry door and raised his Tommy gun. Sir Kuhman and I were sitting ducks. Then "BANG", the goon caught a bullet right between the eyes, he recoiled and spun backwards through the door he had just come out of. I turned expecting to see one of our guys. Instead I discovered a huge man that was dressed like a cook. This guy had on all the apparel including the funny cook's hat. He was as big as a tree and looked like a football linebacker. Then with a deep voice that bellowed through the hall he said, "I'm agent 0008. this way men." We got to our feet and ran down the hall behind him and without losing stride Agent 0008 burst through a locked door. He turned to Sir Kuhman and me and said, "This is the way to the casino. I'm sure you two would like a place at the craps table right?"

I was astonished, when I say Agent 0008 burst through the door. I mean he smashed straight through a locked door without opening it like it was made of balsa wood instead of oak. We went down a set of stairs and as we reached the bottom another gangster sprung out of a doorway pointing his gun. BANG, Agent 0008 shot him right through his forehead. "Sir Kuhman," I remarked, "I think we have found a highly qualified escort. I wonder if he can really cook." When we hit the landing we turned right stepping over the body lying there and went down a short dark hallway. Agent 0008 stopped us and said, "Stand ready. I'll take out the door." Agent 0008 ran the hall and slid as if going into third base. He kicked the door breaking the lock and the doorjamb holding it, the door ripped open. I went in first and then Sir Kuhman. We had our guns raised expecting we'd be shot at as soon as we stepped into the room. To our pleasant surprise we found about 80 men and woman sitting on the floor with their hands on their heads. A door opened at the far end of the room and a sleazy looking man stepped out. In an instant Sir Kuhman raised his gun ready to shoot the guy.

The sleazy looking guy also pulled his gun up and as Sir Kuhman was pulling the trigger Agent 0008 quickly lifted Sir

Kuhman's arm and the gun went off into the ceiling. "Gentlemen meet Agent OOLX." "Why did you shoot at me?" asked agent OOLX. "Did I do something wrong sir? Isn't this the way you wanted these wonderfully dressed gamblers and socialites, all wrapped up with a ribbon and bow?" He let out a hardy laugh. "You scared the life out of me," said Sir Kuhman. Sorry for taking a shot at you." "That's okay old chap," said Agent OOLX after hearing Sir Kuhman's English accent. "I hope you didn't shoot the bloody toes off anyone upstairs. Off with you now. I'll keep this group in check and you chaps head upstairs. Cheerio," Agent OOLX chuckled.

So we headed upstairs to see if they had captured Big Barney. The gunfire had all subsided by the time we reached the first floor. A great deal of noise was coming from the patrons in the restaurant. Women were sobbing and the band was hiding on the floor behind the drum set and the piano. About sixty other very frightened women and men were hiding behind the chairs and tables that had all been turned over. One lady was howling so much I shouted to the two officers in charge, "Hey Bobby," He didn't hear me so I yelled his nickname even louder. "RED, hey RED, can't you and Dick get that lady to shut up? If you can't, get her the hell out of here. I can't hear a thing because she's squealing so damn loud." Red answered back, "It's not a lady sir, it's a man." Just then this big dude got up wiping his eyes and whimpered, "Please let me go. I just came for the catch of the day." "Let him go sit in the back of your police car," yelled Sir Kuhman, "and give him a handkerchief."

Everything was in control so Sir Kuhman and I left to head towards Big Barney's office and crossed paths with Agent Rigoni who was coming down the hallway from some other part of the building. Chief Swetz was already talking to Big Barney through his office door. He queried Agent Rigoni to see if he wanted to take over the dialog with Big Barney. Rigoni said no and stood aside. Chief Swetz continued to talk to Big Barney but it was hard to do so through a locked steel door, "Big Barney, who's in there with you?" "It's just me and my brothers. We'll come out peaceable like, just give us a few minutes to prepare." "You got one minute Big Barney and then we'll blow a hole through the wall with enough dynamite to send you and your brothers to Kingdom Come." "Okay we're ready to come out," yelled Big Barney. It was then we heard a motor start. "What's that noise coming from inside the room?" asked Chief Swetz. As he finished his sentence a huge explosion was heard, the hallway we were standing in started filling up with smoke and dust. One of Chief Swetz men yelled in, "Big Barney's getting away. He blew the wall out in the back of the building and it dropped down to create a ramp and Big Barney drove his car right out of the building. He's heading south on Culver Road and we never got off a shot." Chief Swetz yelled, "Is Officer Schirmer okay? He was assigned to watch that side of the building." "Yes sir, he's fine but unfortunately was unable to stop them. He was too busy dodging pieces of the wall as it fell down."

We all took off for our cars and raced down Culver Road. One of Chief Swetz's men was waiting at the corner of

Durand Boulevard directing us to follow Big Barney through the park. We spun around the corner and sped down the road as fast as our vehicles would take us. As we drove past the bathhouse on the lake the rain started coming down exceptionally hard and the wind was picking up. I could see a train coming down the Hojack Line. Its headlight lit up enough of the area that we could see Big Barney's car way off in the distance. We were gaining on him but he had a huge head start. We lost track of him when he turned onto Saint Paul Boulevard and we were sure he was heading towards the harbor on the west side of the Genesee River. He must have a ship along the river front docks. As we approached the Stutson Street Bridge we noticed one of the orange globe fire alarm boxes had been knocked over. Big Barney must have done it to try to set off the alarm and choke the roads with fire equipment. Chief Swetz slowed and signaled to his officers to head towards Lake Avenue. We turned north down River Street but saw fire engines pulling out of Station 22. The police cars got around them before they blocked the road. Agent Rigoni was behind us, he also went towards Lake Avenue. Assuming Big Barney headed for the harbor everyone was now converging near the lake. Police cars were on every conceivable approach route and we all joined up near the Charlotte pier. Chief Swetz opened his door and shouted, "Did anyone see them? Have we got anything? Has anyone spotted them since turning off Stutson Street?" Everyone signaled no. "Where the hell did they go? I can't believe we lost them. They must have turned south on Lake

Ave." I asked the Chief, "Have you got cars patrolling from Ridge Road down?" "Yes, Captain August. I also alerted all of the local police agencies. Everyone is out in force and watching all the main escape routes." "Then don't worry we'll find them, they can't get too far," said Sir Kuhman. Just as we were about to head back up Lake Avenue one of Chief Swetz guys pulled up and yelled, "Chief we have them cornered. Big Barney turned at Boxart Street and he was driving towards a dead end." "Let's go," yelled Chief Swetz. "No wait Chief. Stop," I shouted back. "He's not stupid enough to get himself trapped there. He must have a cruiser or a speedboat stashed some place on the river near the end of Boxart Street. Let's get to the Coast Guard station and get ready. If he has an escape plan you can bet he'll be going by the station and very soon. Chief, your men can handle the situation on Boxart Street. If he really is trapped there he won't get away." So Agent Rigoni, Chief Swetz, Sir Kuhman and I all started towards the Coast Guard Station situated on the east side of the Genesee River. As we got to the station I ordered the cutter readied and fueled immediately. If they got by us and got out on the lake we'd lose them in the rainstorm.

It was only a minute or two and sure enough there they were. Big Barney and his brothers were making headway to the lake at full throttle. Because of the crowd now gathering on the western shore we couldn't shoot for fear any miss would hit civilians. So we all jumped on board and with the cutter only half full we headed out about a half-mile behind them. "Full speed as soon as you can give it to me," I yelled. Then the bow came up and the ship planed off quickly. The wind was picking up and the rain was getting more intense. My mind drifted back to earlier that night and I started thinking about my little friends in Halloween masks. I'm sure they were tucked in their beds for the night and all fast asleep. I hoped they all got in safe with few raindrops on their heads and full sacks of candy.

Keeping site of Big Barney was incredibly difficult. As we hit each wave the mist covered all of us on the bow lookout. Big Barney was making turns to try to shake us off. The waves were getting heavier and the rain was coming down in sheets. We were very close to losing Big Barney when the lightning and thunder started. "Holy Cows," hollered Seaman Kazlukas. "We're going to get fried by a lightning bolt out here." "Kazlukas, stay on course 110 until I tell you to change or I'll send a lightning bolt to fire up your butt, got it?" Seaman Freddie Kazlukas was a funny guy and a friend to everyone, the entire crew thought the world of him. Any other helmsman in the world might have yelled, "Holy Cow" but not our Freddy. It was always, "Holy Cows."

Freddy has a brother John, and I have had the privilege of knowing both of them. As brothers they were like day and night, complete opposites. They were raised in the same home by their grandmother who was a strong disciplinarian. As much as Freddie and his brother John were different I remember how funny it was to hear them talk to each other. Sometimes they'd speak in half sentences yet they'd know exactly what the other was saying. I witnessed it many times. Freddy would say something like, "Hey John remember when grandma did yah know, whoosh," and Freddie would make a gesture. Then John would say, "Yah woe." That was a complete communication between them. It was like code but they both understood the meaning. I served a short stint in the North Atlantic with John when I was in the Navy. John is now Admiral John Kazlukas serving in the South Seas and is commander of a destroyer group. Much bigger, smarter and younger than Freddie, John has a master's degree from the Naval Academy and moved up the leadership rank fast. Freddie spent most of his career dancing up a storm at any and every nearby joint that had music and flappers. Freddie was a smooth talking and fancy dressing man and as a seaman he was fearless. Freddie was also exceptional at the helm, the best in class. Freddie could pilot us through a keyhole and not touch either side.

SNAP, BOOM. A lightning bolt lit up the sky and it was close. Seaman Kazlukas spotted Big Barney and turned course without being ordered too. "Great move helmsman, if you catch site of Big Barney alter course as needed," I exclaimed. I smiled after saying that knowing in my mind he'd do it anyway before receiving orders. One of Freddie's faults is that he does things without waiting for orders. In most cases, that works well and unfortunately doesn't other times. He just can't seem to lose that habit and it has kept his rank rising and falling like a yoyo.

"1st Class Petty Officer Myers, load the forward gun." "Yes Captain, will we be firing over their bow sir?" "No, we don't know what else is out here and I'm not risking hitting the wrong vessel. Target amidships and blow them out of the water. Wait for my command!" "Chief Swetz, please warn them that we are about to fire," "My pleasure sir." Chief Swetz grabbed the megaphone and opened the hatch and then spoke directly to Big Barney. "Big Barney, we are about to fire upon your vessel if you don't stop immediately."

Seconds past and we spotted Big Barney take a quick turn to the right without slowing. "Okay, that's it, we warned them, FIRE." A huge BANG came from the forward gun. We saw it rip through a section of the cruisers upper bridge. Then, SNAP, BOOM, SNAP, BOOM, SNAP BOOM, a string of lightning bolts hit right around Big Barney's cruiser. SNAP BOOM, SNAP BOOM, lightning just hit our ship and knocked a few guys right on their butts, including Seaman Kazlukas. Without a moment's hesitation Freddie was off the floor checking his position and adjusting course faster than he could dance the Charleston. "That was shockingly close sir but I have us on course. I saw Big Barney's cruiser again in the flash and if he hasn't turned we're heading right for him Captain." "Thank you." "1st Class Petty Officer Myers, be ready to fire again on my orders." In the next lightning flash we all caught site of Big Barney and we were right on his tail, 100 to 150 yards and gaining. Before I could give the order to fire we heard SNAP, SNAP, CRACK, BOOM. Lightning struck us again and this time it hit the ships electrical system. Sparks flew from every circuit and we immediately could tell that it knocked out our engines and most of our systems. We were coasting to a dead stop in the water and Big Barney was already out of sight. The rain and wind were giving him a natural veil to hide behind. We were about to lose him for good and there wasn't a damn thing we could do about it. Then inexplicable things began to happen all around us. In many ways I found what we would experience to be remarkable, maybe even miraculous in a strange sort of way. I had never seen anything like it before or since. The clouds seemed to come low and get very thick and black. They started swirling around Big Barney's cruiser and seemed to be holding the ship in place. We could see right through the clouds as they swirled faster and faster. It looked like we were watching a flicker show like the ones at Dreamland Park for a penny. Suddenly bolts of lightning started to rain down, first into the clouds surrounding Big Barney's ship then they moved in on Big Barney's cruiser. It seemed like his cruiser was the only target on the entire lake. We were at a complete stop now and all we could do is watch this amazing spectacle. The clouds seemed to whirl like a small hurricane and they were making a low humming sound like a top spinning. The cruiser seemed to start spinning and the lightning kept hitting it and lighting up the entire craft as if it were a huge glowing light bulb. Then a fog engulfed the ship and the wind increased to over 120 miles per hour and it blew us back almost a mile. Wind, rain, lightning and fog all seemed to gather in one area and then with one huge ROAR a massive lightning bolt hit the entire area encompassing Big Barney's ship and everything disappeared.

The clouds, the rain, the wind, the lightning, all gone, vanished into thin air taking Big Barney's cruiser with it. Sir Kuhman was the first to speak, "Mother Mary, what the hell just happened?" "I'm not sure, my brain is still tingling from the lightning strikes," I replied. Then I asked, "Is everyone all right? Let's get a head count immediately." We concluded that all were present and accounted for. Seaman Kazlukas looked white as a sheep. He exclaimed, "Sir, I think we just witnessed the wrath of God snatching Big Barney and his brothers, and carrying them off. Not much scares me sir but ghosts and acts of God freak me out." I was thinking the same thing, "You're right about that seaman. That was one for the books. If I hadn't witnessed it myself I wouldn't have believed it. No one could escape that lightning storm and I know I've never heard of a cruiser vanishing like that. It must have sunk into the deep, I guess. Perhaps God snatched it and found a place in Hell for those scoundrels." I glanced over at Agent Rigoni and he looked petrified. He was backed into a corner of the bridge and the walls seemed to be propping him up. I asked him if he was feeling all right. He broke his stare just long enough to yell, "Captain August get us out of here right now!" He was panicking, but why? The storm was gone and we were all safe. Sir Kuhman was right when he said he couldn't figure Agent Rigoni out. There is something odd about this guy, and I can't put my finger on it. In any event it was time to head back. I called to Seaman Kazlukas, "Take us about and back to port, great job tonight sailor." Chief Swetz leaned over to me and with a big smile and said, "We now need to place the gangsters and gamblers we caught tonight into jail cells. Other than that, I believe we have wrapped this up." That night ended the Big Barney criminal enterprise era in Irondequoit. However, it didn't end the strange and unbelievable twists and turns of the events that were about to unfold over the next day.

The night and the operation to capture Big Barney was over. We had all the key players and their families gathered at a final celebration. Agent Rigoni took the stage and introduced himself. He smiled and started to speak. "I want to offer my thanks to the operational leaders, Sir Kuhman, Captain August, Chief Swetz and all the men and women of their squads who took part in this remarkably successful operation. I am very grateful for all the work you have done to close a very sad chapter in local history. The FBI thanks you for your partnership and hard work. Now let me introduce Chief Dennis Swetz of the Irondequoit Police."

"Good evening, as Chief of Police in this beautiful small town I haven't had the chance to take part in an operation of this magnitude. I thank God for that. I don't think I want to be in the line of fire again anytime soon. This intensity would eventually give me heart burn." The crowd laughed and applauded. "However, if I hadn't had this stimulating experience I wouldn't be able to stand up here in front of all of you very brave men and women and present these awards. Let me ask the following men to step forward, Special Agent Val Piotrowski, aka Agent 0008, Special Agent

Larry Gartz, aka Agent OOLX, both were sent to us from the New York City FBI Office. I'd also like to ask Lieutenant G. F. Mendoza and Seaman Freddie Kazlukas to step forward.

Gentlemen, each of you represents a special branch of service to our nation. Your extraordinary talents and bravery have added an essential ingredient to the success of this operation. Therefore, it is my honor to present "The Exceptional Merit Award with a Green Star." This award is given for acts of bravery intelligently performed, involving personal risk to life. Congratulations, it has been an honor to work with you and every member of this team."

"Next, I have a special surprise. One hour ago I received a telegram from our Governor Franklin D. Roosevelt. It's a good thing I brought my glasses with me so I will read it." It says, "Congratulations to the men and women of the FBI, the United States Coast Guard, and the Irondequoit Police for your service to our state. It is my honor to award the New York State Governor's Citation to each unit involved in this operation. You are all to be congratulated. Thank you all from the bottom of my heart. You have performed an outstanding service to the Rochester community, signed, Franklin D. Roosevelt." As Chief of Police I want to say this has been one of the proudest days of my life. Thank you and good night."

The speeches were over and a few people headed for the door. Everyone else was milling around eating cake, drinking coffee and saying his or her goodbyes. Even our key informant, Larry Richards, was there. He had been released on his own recognizance and came to join the festivities but stayed mostly in the very back. I doubt he had really been invited, but what the hell, if it hadn't been for him Big Barney might have gotten away with murder. It was such a relief to see this chapter of Irondequoit history close. All the criminals were charged and safe in their cells. Big Barney's distillery, casino, and restaurant were boarded up and closed down. With a final thank you from each of the group leaders the joint operation was declared officially closed. "You're dismissed," were the final words of Agent Rigoni. I said a special goodbye and shook hands with all the out of town team members. It had been an honor to work with them.

The next day started and I was sure everyone involved in the Big Barney operation was heading home or was back into their routine. What I didn't know at the time was that the Big Barney operation wasn't really over. There was more to come and the true end was still heading our way. There was work to do and a mystery to solve but it was all hidden from our eyes.

It was midafternoon and I received a report from one of my patrols that had just rushed in from out on the lake. I immediately grabbed the phone and called Chief Swetz. "Chief Swetz, this is Captain August. You need to get down to my office RIGHT NOW as fast as your car can carry you." Minutes later Chief Swetz pulled in, I could hear his breaks squeal as his car came to an abrupt halt. He rushed inside and right into my office and asked, "What's going on Captain?" "Chief my men were out on routine patrol and they spotted a cruiser that looks remarkably like Big Barney's. Petty Officer Karl was on board and suggested they contact me before boarding the craft." "Great thinking Karl, but how can this be happening? That ship couldn't have survived the storm. We were there and it vanished. How could it still be afloat, how? Where's its location Captain?" "Chief it doesn't really have a stable location. It appears to be coming straight to shore at about 5 knots." "Where will it hit shore Captain?" "If it stays on its current course it will go right down the center of the river." "How the hell can a drifting cruiser head upstream against the river's current, Captain?" "We don't know. It seems to be under power but my men reported they couldn't hear any engines running." "It should be getting closer so let's go out and see if we can spot it."

Chief Swetz and I went outside and walked the river's east shore down to the Coast Guard pier. Sure enough there it was, Big Barney's cruiser heading right up the river. "Seaman Kazlukas, take a small crew on the tug and set a heading parallel to its course but don't get too close. Let's see how far it will go up river." As Big Barney's cruiser approached the front of the Coast Guard Station it started to turn in as if it were being guided to the dock. As it turned back down river, facing the lake, it pulled right up to the Coast Guard dock and just coasted in. I called out, "Quickly tie it up men. Let's make sure she stays put."

Chief Swetz and I were first onboard. We found three dressed skeletons sitting in the galley and a full deck of cards was spread out on the table. Their clothing was identified as being Big Barney's, Neil "the Squeal's", and Felton "the Fiend's", they were nothing but bones. They looked like they were playing a card game. What a vision played out in my mind, three skeletons laughing, drinking, and playing poker as if they were back at Big Barney's.

As others came on board the reaction was shock and fear. A few of the Police and Coast Guardsmen got sick at the site of the boney skeletons and ran out on the deck. Dead fish were all over the floor and deck and many sloshed around in the engine room. The smell was overwhelming.

In Big Barney's stateroom there was a book and a map. The book had all the financial information for Big Barney's business and showed deposits to EC. The map was a bit tough to decipher but it appeared to point the way to a hidden vault on Zoo Road in Durand Park. Chief Swetz, "Do you think we can find this spot based on the few markings on this drawing?" "I sure do Captain. This map might explain why Big Barney donated so much money to the zoo a few years back. This small circle is right off the main road directly in the parks zoo. If I'm looking at this map right this set of lines is where the deer and bison are and the other lines are in the area that includes the elephant exhibit and this circle seems to be right in or next to that exhibit. I'm sure these exhibits were built with a donation by Big Barney and constructed by contractors he hired. He got an award for his philanthropy from the town. That's a great place to hide a stash of money, silver, or gold. No one will be snooping around with an elephant on guard. Perhaps the deposits in the EC could mean Elephant Cage. That sounds like a bit of a stretch but we may be able to find out?"

After completing our search of Big Barney's cruiser and spending a great deal of time on Big Barney's financial records it became very clear that Big Barney had three partners. We knew about only two of them, his two brothers, but who was the third? Now all of a sudden the case we thought we wrapped up last night might not be as wrapped up as we thought. "Okay men; let's get those skeletons to the morgue for formal identification and then I want all of you to report back to my office. Everyone here is ordered to keep all we found here quiet till further notice. Did you hear that order men?" Chief Swetz required a very strong YES SIR from everyone onboard before they were allowed to disembark.

Chief Swetz and I headed back to his office where we devised a plan to set a trap to see if we could find out who the third partner was. Chief Swetz gave an interview to Rochester's top newspaper reporters Dan Alhart and Jan Flasch. Chief Swetz told them what our plan was and promised exclusive access to this story when concluded. Both Hart and Flasch agreed that our best hope was to plant a story on the front page of that night's Times Union. It would say that the police found a map in Big Barney's cruiser with a note saying that Big Barney had hidden something in Durand Park, perhaps a body. The article revealed that the map found in Big Barney's cruiser was damaged but that it appeared to be in the area of the picnic pavilions or possibly in the area of the zoo. The article also stated that police were planning to start the search near the picnic pavilions. If nothing was found they would then proceed to the zoo area the next day. The search would include digging and probing areas around the picnic pavilions and a similar process at the zoo. We did not release information that we suspected that the map might lead to a vault of money or valuables or that Big Barney might have another partner. The misinformation planted in the newspaper was put there to scare any unknown partner of Big Barney's into acting quickly. The plan published only allowed a one day window to get to the zoo area ahead of us, assuming they existed and were still alive.

That night, hours after the story hit the streets, Chief Swetz and I with a few top officers gathered to stakeout an area across from the elephant exhibit. It was our hope that the third partner would show up to open the vault in advance of our search. As promised we allowed news reporters Dan Alhart and Jan Flasch to be on hand to document what we were all hoping would be a big story and not a bust. We were about to give up when Jan Flasch thought she noticed some movement in the gorge. Then one of the officers signaled that they heard something.

Creeping up from the gorge on the backside of the elephant cage was a person dressed in very dark clothing. As soon as they approached the cage the Chief gave the signal to turn on our spotlights. Chief Swetz yelled out "HALT IN THE NAME OF THE LAW, PUT YOUR HANDS UP AND DROP YOUR WEAPON." The dark figure turned and started to rush back to the edge of the gorge. Chief Swetz shot a warning shot over his head and again yelled "HALT!" The dark figure turned and fired a semi-automatic pistol he had and a spray of bullets hit above us crack, crack, crack, crack. The dark figure fired too high or we'd have casualties for sure. At that point every policeman started shooting at the shadowy figure.

The shadowy figure took so many bullets all at once it blew them backwards down the gorge. Chief Swetz yelled, "Stop firing!" When all the guns fell silent we all ran to the top of the gorge. With flashlights we could see the shadowy figure at the bottom of the gorge was dead for sure. The Tommy gun he had fired was lying far behind him and blood was all over the body. We all rushed down the hill but before we got to the bottom Chief Swetz held out his arms and motioned to us to stop. He shouted, "Not too close boys, this is a crime scene and I'd like to preserve it as best we can." Everyone formed a circle around the person lying there dead. Their jacket was torn apart from all the bullet holes in it and blood was all over the body. Chief Swetz walked up and slowly rolled the body over, dirt, old leaves and blood obscured the face. Chief Swetz grabbed a handkerchief from his pocket to wipe the face off to reveal the identity. There were a few gasps from the men as Chief Swetz revealed that the face was none other than Special Agent Gary W. Rigoni. As conversation broke out we all struggled to understand what we were seeing. One officer asked a question, not to any one person, but to all those present. "Is this a terrible mistake of some kind?" Chief Swetz spoke up, "He had a gun, we gave him an opportunity to give up, and he shot at us. This was no mistake, and thinking back this explains many inconsistencies in his behaviors.

Sir Kuhman was the first to mention to me that there was something odd afoot. We opened an investigation into Agent Rigoni to learn more about him. Did greed drive him in search for Big Barney's treasure? Was he in partnership with Big Barney? What drove him to turn into a criminal? See the epilogue below. The answer surprised us but explained everything. The day after Agent Rigoni was killed we searched for Big Barney's hidden loot we were sure existed. It was never found.

The End...

Epilogue:

<u>Who was agent Gary W. Rigoni?</u>

Special Agent Gary W. Rigoni turned out to be the missing brother of Big Barney, Neil "the Squeal", and Felton "the Fiend". He also turned out to be very, very dead when he was checked out by Coast Guard medics Nicky and Adele at the bottom of the gorge. An autopsy was never done. It was assumed that the 32 bullets in his body were most likely the cause of his demise. When interrogated one of Big Barney's thugs admitted that it was Agent Rigoni that was tipping off his brother. Big Barney however didn't think he was doing enough to help. Therefore, as we surrounded Big Barney's, Big Barney was ordering one of his men to make the first shot count and kill Agent Rigoni. He tried to kill his own brother, but he missed. The Irondequoit Police didn't.

<u>No hanging for Big Barney</u>.

Although a few of Big Barney's men did hang, Big Barney himself managed to avoid the hangman noose. Everyone involved felt Big Barney did get what he deserved in the end. Big Barney and his brothers were erased from earth by some unknown force as if they never existed.

<u>Where did the loot go?</u>

Uncle Neil told me that they spent many hours trying to find the vault and whatever might be in it but they were unsuccessful. It's a mystery why Big Barney's stash was never found. Agent Rigoni did not risk coming to the zoo to take a walk in the dark. He had to be there to unbury the riches his brother had buried. It's true that the map that was found was not clear and the vaults hiding place was never really pinpointed. The Zoo that existed at that time and for many more years made it hard for anyone to search in earnest. It has since passed into Rochester history. Perhaps some deserving person will unearth the treasure some day in the future.

Life goes on in and out of prison.

When the arrests of the dirty cops finally came the younger officers did their best to protect their fathers but all went to jail. I heard that after getting out of jail years later the boys moved to Ft. Worth, Texas and started a cement business called "Three Ways Concrete." They have not been heard from since. Uncle Neil would joke that they most likely went into business with the mob making cement shoes. Their fathers went their separate ways.

Jim Trescott changed his name to Edward Kramer and moved to New York City. He always wanted to become a banker. He tried to commit suicide when he was turned down by Dime Bank and S. Heads Bank. He recovered but was then seriously injured falling off ball washer he tried to stand during a local golf tournament when intoxicated. He joined AAA and became a recovering alcoholic. Finally he got a job at the Buffalo State Bank to fulfill his dream. Years later the police tried to arrest him for embezzlement and was killed in a police shootout.

The other father Mike Rhodes became very involved in the church. Later he went on a long sabbatical that included an around the world cruise. Upon his return he became leader of a church in Gates, New York. I heard that he dedicated his life to helping the poor and needy. The belief is that he had made a promise to St. Jude while in prison that he'd follow a righteous path and he did.

Sir Kuhman went on to head many special operations for the FBI and Scotland Yard and was awarded the Presidential Medal of Freedom by President Herbert Hoover. Over the years he took up the game of golf as suggested by many friends. Upon his retirement he dedicated much more time to his love of the game of golf. He joined Timber Ridge Golf Club, an elite golf course near Rochester, New York. Sir Kuhman and Chief Swetz became great friends, yet golf rivals and competed against each other in many championships.

Chief Swetz became head of the New York State Police and had a very distinguished career. Chief Swetz lacked the golf talent Sir Kuhman had nevertheless he dominated the winner's circle. His one vice as a casual gambler gave him the edge to overcome the intense anxieties known for taking down great golfers when under pressure. Although his ball often strayed into the trees he was a fearless tiger in the woods.

Edward August purchased a home and retired with my wife, Kathy, to a small town, Estero, Florida. It was his hope to become a professional senior golfer. Lacking skill in golf he had to settle for becoming a ranger on a newly built country club named Pelican Sound. This beautiful community became the home of the world's best senior golfers. It was the perfect place to retire.

Seek and ye shall find! Places mentioned in this book can still be visited.

LDR's Char Pit is one of the great ones. LDR's is one of the best places on earth to stop for breakfast, lunch, or dinner. Filled with photos from the turn of the 20th century people travel from all over to eat their charbroiled favorites. Try the Charbroiled Steak Sandwich, a Cheeseburger or Hamburger the favorite of Agent Piotrowski. Edward August's favorite is a hotdog on a grilled hard roll but he needs a minimum of one bottle of catchup. Top any of these off with one of their famous milkshakes and you're in heaven.

Dreamland now Seabreeze Amusement Park is an exceptional family fun spot. The merry-go-round, Jack Rabbit, Bumper Cars and Water Fun Park, make for a fabulous day for the family. There are so many great attractions at Seabreeze I'd have to write book to mention them all. Take your family for a day of fun.

Fire Station 22 is now an exceptional restaurant. This is another great place to eat and drink and a great destination restaurant. Many photos and pieces of firehouse memorabilia are on hand to add to the experience.

Salem United Church of Christ where the Pundt funerals were held is still open on Bittner Street near the inner loop. This church has to be one of the most attractive places to worship in the city of Rochester. Stop in some Sunday for church and then ask for a tour. You'll love it. I attended a candlelight wedding at the church years ago. It was truly the most beautiful wedding I ever attended.

The Irondequoit Police Department is still on Titus Ave. The Irondequoit Police were one of the great memory builders of our youth as sponsor of "Kiddy Fun Day" at Seabreeze Amusement Park. "Kiddy Fun Day" was only one of the many services provide to Irondequoit citizens over the years by this exceptional Police force.

Big Barney's Speakeasy was inspired by a historic and favored restaurant and bar "The Reunion Inn" known as a treasured gathering spot on Culver Road in Sea Breeze, New York. The Reunion Inn was a stop on the Underground Railroad, as well as a speakeasy during Prohibition. Stop by for a casual lunch, dinner, or a drink at the bar. You can visit this wonderful old establishment almost any day of the year. Say hi to the owners Jim Barnash or Steve Sahs. Mention that Big Barney sent you and maybe they'll give you a discount on a depression era beer. Watch out for the ghosts that haunt the Inn. They have been known for tripping people in the halls then laughing when they fall and spill their beer. These troublesome spirits can be heard whispering to each other in dark corners.

Peter Pundt's Yacht, "Dill" and Big Barney's Cruiser were inspired by two ships that can be viewed from the tow path walkway along the Genesee River not far up the river from the O'Rorke Bridge. The ship we renamed "Dill" has deteriorated over the years as one would expect. The ship we called Big Barney's cruiser is very easy to spot. You'll see the severe damage caused by lightning strikes. I have no doubt that the ghosts of the past still visit these ships. I'm sure ghosts can be heard and seen in the still of the night.

Some places mentioned in this book were well known in years past but are now gone from the Rochester landscape. The Hub Theater was the place to go to see the most recent movies but is now a gas station and store. The Coal Towers are gone now they were near the end of Irondequoit Bay just a half mile before you get to Oklahoma Beach on the lake side.

The Hojack Railroad Line is gone but pieces of it can still be found rusting but otherwise untouched by time all along the edge of Lake Ontario from Hilton to Webster, New York and beyond.

Are Ghosts Real?

Join the GHOST WALK of Sea Breeze. You may see the spirits of former slaves and others walking about, or the ghost of speakeasy owner Neil Steimer. As you proceed, look in the top floor windows at the Sea Breeze Fire Department. Many are certain that the ghost of a Fire Chief from long ago still walks the upper floors and watches over the neighborhood. To learn more about what Sea Breeze has to offer, ask the wonderful people at the Reunion Inn for more information about the ghost walk.

Prohibition Era Beer at Rohrbach's !

Uncle Neil loved the taste of prohibition era beer. He said the best beer sold today couldn't compare. He thought the taste of prohibition beer couldn't be duplicated because it came with the thrill of getting it when beer was illegal. He changed his mind when I took him to the Rohrbach Brewing Company. His eyes lit up and he asked me jokingly, "Did they make this in the back room?" He didn't know that they really made the beer on site. He never heard about a microbrewery that someone wasn't trying to hide. Even when he was in the nursing home he'd ask me to sneak in some of what he called "The Special Rohrbach Beer".

Prohibition Ended December 5, 1933

The 21st Amendment to the U.S. Constitution is ratified, repealing the 18th Amendment and bringing an end to the era of national prohibition of alcohol in America. At 5:32 p.m. EST, Utah became the 36th state to ratify the amendment, achieving the requisite three-fourths majority of states' approval. Pennsylvania and Ohio had ratified it earlier in the day.

Thank you for reading this book. My new book can be purchased on line at Amazon Books. It is about a young man facing life in the Civil War era and it's called.

"One Bullet to Manhood" "One Bullet to Destiny"

Any questions or to purchase a signed copy of any of my books please email me at snapusa@rochester.rr.com.

****

To my wife Kathy and daughters Kara and Dawn,

This book is dedicated to you. If I wrote a book about how much I love you and how proud I am of you it would make War and Peace look thin. What a wonderful adventure my life is because of you three. Plus look at the fabulous son-in-law's and beautiful grandchildren you have added. I sure have been blessed.